JOURNEY
Back to Christmas

Based on the Hallmark Channel Original Movie
Written By Marie Nation

Leigh Duncan

ISBN: 978-1-947892-10-1

www.hallmarkpublishing.com
For more about the movie visit:
www.hallmarkmoviesandmysteries.com/journey-back-to-christmas

Table Of Contents

Chapter One

December, 1945

Her purse meticulously balanced in her lap, Hanna Morse crossed her ankles and pushed down a quiver of anticipation as the heavy curtains pulled away from the movie screen. She aimed a brave smile at the tall brunette sitting beside her, glad she'd let Dottie talk her into coming to the theater tonight. Moping around the house certainly wasn't doing her any good.

It had been six months since that terrible day when the telegram arrived. Six months, and she still couldn't make it through the day—or the night—without tears.

But tonight, she'd let Dottie convince her to take in a picture show. While she'd never get over the pain of losing Chet, she needed to escape her grief just for a little while. To laugh, to enjoy life. At least, long enough to watch a movie.

Lights flickered on the screen. Hanna straightened. Dottie had promised the movie was a good one—a comedy starring Frank Sinatra and Gene Kelly. It had been so long since she'd laughed out loud that she'd nearly forgotten what her own laughter sounded like. Looking forward to it, she let herself relax.

But instead of the opening credits, the screen filled with images of soldiers marching through New York City. Unprepared, Hanna tensed as the voice of the newscaster filled the theater.

"New York pays tribute to the American foot soldier. These men were chosen to represent all the ten million soldiers of the United States Army. Gliders fly overhead as the city roars its welcome home to the thirteen thousand veterans who fought from Sicily and Italy through Normandy, Holland and Germany. Four million New Yorkers line the four-and-a-half-mile parade route to greet the men…"

She pressed shaky fingers beneath her eyes, straightened her shoulders, and took a breath. She could do this. She could sit here while the boys—everyone else's boys—marched beneath the ticker tape thrown from tall buildings while crowds cheered. She could keep a smile on her face while wives and mothers welcomed husbands and sons home from the war. Chet would expect her to do that much. He'd be the first to remind her that others had sacrificed far more than she had. He'd tell her to think about the Sullivan family and all they'd lost. He'd…

But Chet wasn't here. He wasn't among those who were coming home.

And she wasn't that strong.

Abruptly, she stood. Thankful she and Dottie had chosen seats on the aisle, she grabbed her coat and hat and headed for the lobby. As she rushed up the aisle, plush carpet silenced the sound of the black pumps she'd bought especially for this night, her first night out in half a year. The swinging doors opened into a lobby filled with twinkling Christmas lights and bright red ribbons. The decorations announced the happiness of the season. She blinked, struggling against her tears. She thought she had a pretty good chance of winning the battle over her emotions until a whiff of pine from the boughs that hung over the doors and around the window sills reminded her of Chet. The mask of cheery goodwill she did her best to maintain threatened to collapse completely.

Why, oh why, had she agreed to go out with Dottie tonight? She had no business being here. She needed to go home, to lose herself in memories of better times, of better days. Lately, it was the only way she ever got through the long, lonely nights. Even then, she slept in fits and starts. When she did manage to drift off, she dreamed of Chet dying on a field in a foreign country with no one there to comfort him.

Tears stung her eyes in earnest now. Fighting them, she slipped her arms into her coat. She had to leave.

Dottie caught up to her before she made it halfway across the lobby.

She turned to the woman who'd been the best friend a girl could ever ask for during those first, awful days after she'd received the news. "Oh, Dottie," she said, tugging on her gloves. "I don't want you to miss out because of me. Go back inside and watch the movie. I'll be all right. I just…" She sniffled.

"I wouldn't dream of staying without you." Sympathy glinted in Dottie's dark eyes. She overrode Hanna's protest while she put on her own coat. Together, they hurried toward the exit. "Oh, Hanna, I didn't know there'd be a newsreel." Dottie's breath spiraled into a cloud the instant she stepped from the warmth of the theater onto the sidewalk. Behind her, colorful Christmas lights outlined posters of the coming attractions.

"It's not your fault." Hanna stabbed at her tears with gloved fingers that did little more than smear the dampness onto her cheeks, where they froze faster. "Silly me, I… I just, ah…"

"Here." Always prepared, Dottie handed her an embroidered handkerchief she'd pulled from her purse.

Hanna swallowed a sob. Dottie was so kind. Far kinder than a weak-willed woman like her deserved. What was wrong with her? Why couldn't she be stronger? Why couldn't she bury her sorrow and pain? Chet had willingly fought for their country. He was the one who, like so many others, had given his life protecting their freedom while she'd stayed home to watch and wait and support the war effort by buying bonds and saving tin foil. Yet, here she was, in tears again.

Standing in the cold in front of the theater wasn't going to help her get past this, but a walk might clear her head. Mindful of the beautiful but treacherous ice and snow, she started down the sidewalk toward her car with Dottie—bless her—at her side.

She whispered, "I just miss him."

"Of course you do," Dottie agreed.

"Seeing all those soldiers coming home. It just, ah, it breaks me up." She twisted the handkerchief in her hands.

"Of course it does." Dottie leaned down, her voice growing fainter when two women passed them headed in the opposite direction on the sidewalk. "He's your husband."

"Was," Hanna corrected. She had to remember that Chet was gone. Otherwise, a fresh wave of grief would wash over her whenever she thought of him.

"Oh, Hanna, honey. He's still your husband. Nothing changes that."

If only that were true.

More tears hovered near the surface. Any second now, they'd burst through the protective barriers she'd erected around her heart. She tore her gaze from the rooster tail of slush and snow that trailed the tires of a passing car and cast a pleading glance at the friend who was trying so hard to make her feel better.

"Well, you know what I mean." Dottie struggled to offer the right words. "He's still in your heart. You're always going to be Mrs.—" Hanna's expression must have finally registered. "Oh, I'm just making it worse, now, aren't I?"

A muffled sob escaped. The dam broke, and the hot tears ran in rivulets down her cold cheeks.

"Go on and blow." Offering the same kind of advice she'd give one of their patients, Dottie motioned to the handkerchief. She patted the side of a well-stocked purse. "I've got another one in here."

Though her eyes swam, Hanna smiled. No matter how bad things got, she could always count on Dottie to make her laugh. She'd discovered that the day they'd both begun nursing school. They'd been best friends ever since.

"Oh, look at me blubbering." Hanna struggled to pull herself together. "And when all our boys are over there doing something heroic."

"Aw, have a good cry." Dottie patted her shoulder. "Not all of us are born to change the world."

"Yes, but nothing ever got solved by blubbering on a sidewalk, either." That was it, wasn't it? Now, with Chet gone, what use was she? "I'm lost, Dottie," she admitted. "I used to know who I was. I was Mrs. Chet Morse, wife." She sighed. The yellow telegram hadn't just announced Chet's death. In a way, it had marked the end of her life, too. "I wasn't out to change the world. I just wanted to make a happy home for my husband. And now..." She shook her head.

Now, what?

"I don't have any purpose at all." There, she'd said it. Without Chet, without a husband to make a home for, without children to raise, what was she supposed to do with the rest of her life?

"Well," Dottie tilted her head, "you could walk me to the square."

The suggestion was so surprising that she *tsked*. "That's not exactly a purpose."

"You never know." Dottie smiled slyly. "Even the smallest stone makes a ripple in the water."

Hanna glanced at her friend. She didn't understand what Dottie meant and let her eyebrows bunch. "What stone?"

"It's a saying," Dottie answered with a laugh. "C'mon. They're decorating the gazebo."

Well, she'd wanted to take a walk, she conceded while Dottie threaded their arms together. Maybe her friend was right. A walk past Henderson's Hardware and down Main Street to the gazebo might perk her right up. It couldn't hurt to wander past the Christmas trees the shop owners had erected with such care along the sidewalks. Or to take in all the decorations. Everywhere she looked, greenery tied with bright red ribbons gave windows and storefronts a festive look. The colorful lights against the backdrop of a night sky added such a merry touch that they warmed even her heart. Throughout Central Falls, people were trying so hard to make this a cheerful Christmas homecoming for the soldiers and sailors who'd been away at war.

How could she do any less?

By the time she and Dottie reached the center of town, she'd dried her eyes and banished her tears. She even hummed along when Dottie, hearing the carolers on the square, burst into song. As they approached the gazebo, she squared her shoulders and hid her pain. She refused to dampen the mood of her neighbors who were pitching in to decorate the gathering place at the heart of Central Falls. To prove she'd caught the Christmas spirit, she pulled her camera from her bag and snapped a photo of the women in winter coats and heels who busied themselves untangling strings of lights, while men in suits and hats threaded the strands through hooks attached to the gazebo's eaves. Spotting a former patient, she stopped to say hello.

"How are you doing, Mr. McGregor?" She watched closely, ready to spring into action, as the older gentleman wearing a bowler hat leaned from a tall ladder to place an ornament on the Christmas tree. Mr. McGregor had taken a bad fall last year and broken his collarbone. She knew it still gave him fits. "How's your shoulder these days?"

"Ah, you know. The old rheumatism acts up when there's a storm coming." Carefully, Mr. McGregor worked his way down the rungs of the ladder. Once he had both feet on the floor of the gazebo again, he rubbed his arm. "And I can tell there's a doozy coming in tomorrow."

Hanna nodded. At the hospital this afternoon, she'd overheard sweet old Doc Smithy talking with her favorite patient about a blizzard. "That's what everyone's saying."

Mr. McGregor glanced up as if he could see

through the gazebo's pitched roof. "It's a shame, too. Cloud cover is going to hide the comet."

"Oh, darn," Hanna exclaimed with an unexpected pang of disappointment. "I didn't think of that. I was looking forward to seeing it." She shrugged. There were worse things than not seeing a bright light arc across the sky. "But, a big snow storm. It'll be a good night to nestle in, I guess."

Or it would be if she had someone to nestle in with.

She shook the thought aside. Maintaining a brave face, she drew in a steadying breath and issued herself a stern reminder to stay cheerful and upbeat.

But Mr. McGregor only pinned her with a concern that saw through her false bravado. "And how are you holding up?"

Heat flooded her cheeks. Her act wasn't fooling anyone, not if Mr. McGregor's rheumy eyes could see through it. Determined to try harder to do her part, she mustered a smile. "Oh, now, don't you go worrying about me."

"Someone's got to, Nurse Hanna," the old man protested. "You're always taking care of the rest of us."

Genuine warmth deepened her smile. Though she and Chet had talked about moving to the city, people like Mr. McGregor made her glad they'd decided to settle down in Central Falls.

"You'll come to the lighting tomorrow evening, right?" he asked.

The tradition had always been one of the season's

highlights. Dressed in their winter finest, practically everyone in town would gather at the square. In the past, she'd enjoyed watching the children, so eager with anticipation that their eyes sparkled while their little feet danced in the snow. There would be caroling and hot chocolate. Some of the younger boys might even have a snowball fight. How could she miss that? Suddenly her plan to spend another evening all alone didn't seem like such a good one. "Oh, I suppose so," she agreed. "I always like seeing the whole town come out for it."

Mr. McGregor studied the gray skies overhead. "Let's just hope the snow holds off."

The words "yes, let's" were on the tip of her tongue. Before she had a chance to say them, though, Dottie rushed over, holding the enormous silver star that would soon grace the top of the gazebo. Holding it up to her face, the brunette struck a silly pose. Hanna had just enough time to snap a picture before they both laughed.

Coming here was a good thing, she decided as she watched her friend act the clown. After all, they said laughter was the best medicine, and Dottie had given them all a healthy dose of it.

Chapter Two

*L*ate the next day, Hanna exited the ward and headed down a narrow corridor with a metal tray, careful not to jostle the medicines and supplies arranged on it in precise lines. She stepped aside to let an approaching nurse and patient pass through the door ahead of her. While she waited, she took a second to admire the cheery red streamers that swooped in loops along the white walls. Below them, greenery and garlands of red flowers decorated the dark wainscoting. A sharp, clean scent of evergreen drifted in the air, bringing the smells of Christmas to the patients unlucky enough to have to spend their holiday at the Franklin County Hospital.

At the nurses' station, she settled her tray onto the counter and brushed a hand over the starched white pinafore she wore over a blue shirtwaist. The simple gesture pleased her, and she smiled. She loved working at the hospital, bringing hope and care to those who were in need. She adjusted the nursing pin she wore with pride at her shoulder and glanced across the room in time to see her friend, Julia, turn away from the sink.

Catching her eye, Julia raised one hand to her chest. A small diamond sparkled on the ring finger of her left hand. She gave Hanna a shy smile.

"Julia!" Hanna gasped. "He proposed?" She looked about quickly. The patients needed their rest. It wouldn't do to upset them, not even with good news.

"Just now." A soft giggle escaped Julia's mouth despite the hand she held over it.

Barely able to contain herself, Hanna clasped her friend's fingers. "I'm the first to know?"

"You had to be," Julia exclaimed, her voice a throaty whisper. "You're the one who introduced us. If it weren't for you…"

Hanna's smile widened until her face threatened to split in two. She'd known, just known, Julia and Frank were meant for each other the day he'd been transferred here. She stepped back, enjoying a ripple of happiness for the couple. Had they set a date? "Oh, Julia! When?"

"Come." Julia hooked their arms together. "Frank's just bustin' to tell you himself."

Leaving her tray where it was for the moment, Hanna let herself be pulled along. The rubber soles of their shoes squeaking on the polished linoleum squares, the two nurses hurried across the men's ward. They stopped at a bed where an injured vet lay, his head propped up on pillows, his leg in traction. Though he had to be in pain, the soldier had never complained—not even once—during his long stay in the hospital.

While Julia sank onto the bedside chair, Hanna gave Frank's hand a squeeze. "This all happened so fast," she gushed. "I'm so happy for you."

"I asked myself, 'why wait?'" Frank explained. A broad smile softened his thin features. "As soon as I can carry her over the threshold, we're gonna find the closest justice of the peace." He gave his brand-new fiancée a tender smile. "Right, honey?"

Julia slipped Frank's hand in hers. Her face radiant, she fanned herself. "Engaged on the night of the Christmas Comet. Isn't that the most romantic thing?"

Agreeing that it was, Hanna pulled her camera from one of the deep pockets in her pinafore. She couldn't let the precious moment pass by without recording it for posterity. "Look this way, you two lovebirds," she cooed. She snapped the photo of the couple who were perfect for each other. Smiling, she tucked the camera back into her pocket.

"And I'm going to find her a white dress just like the one I saw in a window when I was over there in Italy." Frank squeezed Julia's hand. "Prettiest dress I ever saw," he finished brightly.

"Frank has been telling me all about Italy." Julia bit her lower lip. For an instant, her face fell. They'd all seen pictures of the destruction caused by the war. She rallied quickly. "Well, the good things, anyway.

Hundred-year-old churches and the cobblestone streets…"

"Pretty as a picture, some of those towns." For a second, Frank's eyes glazed over, and he fell silent. Memories moved their icy fingers across his face. He shivered and tugged his Army jacket closer around his shoulders as if saying to himself, *Enough of that.* "But nothin' beats bein' back home."

Julia's gaze dropped to where Frank's fingers were entwined in hers as if she wanted to let him know she understood how much the moment had cost her soon-to-be husband. Though she never voiced the *I'm so glad you made it home*, her thoughts echoed loudly through the room.

Hanna felt her own grief rear its ugly head. She retreated a step. "I, I should be getting to work." Suddenly missing Chet, she plastered a brave smile over her own feelings. "Congratulations, you two. I'm so happy for you." Beating a hasty retreat lest her sorrow ruin Frank and Julia's happy occasion, she headed for the exit.

"Hanna," Julia called before she made it past the third bed.

With a sigh, she turned in time to catch the worried look on her friend's face.

"Oh, Hanna, I wasn't thinking. Here we are, so giddy, and I wasn't even—"

"No, don't apologize, Julia," Hanna insisted. "We've got to keep our eyes on tomorrow, right? That's where happiness is. Not the past." Someday, somehow, she'd find happiness in her future, too. Maybe it wouldn't be the same as she'd had with Chet, but one day, she'd find a purpose in her life.

Julia inhaled a deep breath. "You're such a brave thing," she gushed while something like awe shone in her eyes.

Hanna held up a hand. "I'm not so brave. Just…" She paused. "Just happy to see you so happy." For emphasis, she added, "Really."

Whatever she'd said must have done the trick, because Julia relaxed. The smile she'd worn ever since Hanna had introduced her to Frank warmed her eyes. "We *are* happy," she said on a sigh. "Thanks to you."

"Well…" Hanna slipped her hands into her pockets. "And now, I really do need to get back to work before the head nurse notices I'm missing." Without giving Julia a chance to protest, this time she headed across the ward at a fast clip. Work, she needed to work. Needed to keep her hands busy and her mind focused on taking care of the patients who were too sick or too hurt to spend Christmas at home.

And she knew just which patients needed her most.

Time dragged during the long afternoons in the children's ward. In the mornings, the hospital bustled with activity. Doctors made their rounds. Orderlies and nurses rushed about delivering medicine and changing linens. There were sponge baths to get and clean pajamas to don. Later, visiting hours brightened the early part of the afternoon. But toward the end of the day, things quieted around the hospital. Footfalls echoed in silent halls. And the children grew restless.

The image of a sad-eyed waif who'd fallen from his bunk bed at the Children's Home surfaced, and Hanna's heart went out to the little boy who had lost both his parents far too early. She stopped by the nurses' station long enough to empty her tray, careful to store the medicines and supplies in their assigned places. Retrieving two books from a cubby, she headed for the other side of the hospital.

Toby's face brightened when she approached the bed where the little boy sat, his arm awkward in its heavy cast. She ran one finger across the metal rail at the foot of his bed, checking for dust. Her finger came away clean, and she smiled, satisfied that the area was as neat and tidy as the rest of the hospital.

"I have a few minutes before the end of my shift," she told him. "I picked out some good stories to read." She held out the books she'd chosen from the library cart earlier that day. When the move failed to generate much enthusiasm, she paused to think. What would interest an eight-year-old boy? Sure she'd hit on a good idea, she reached into her pocket. "Would you like to look at my camera while I read to you?"

Toby's eyes lit up. "You have a camera? I'd like to see it very much, Nurse Hanna."

She handed the slim box to the polite child without hesitation. Settling in the chair beside his bed, she read while Toby pretended to snap pictures. "On the left side of her, she presently spied a little wooden hut painted blue and something rose-colored was tied to the handle of its shut blue door. 'A bunch of roses,' said the fairy godmother. And she thought of going over and smelling their sweetness. But when she came close to it…" Hanna looked up from the book. The most exciting part of the story was just ahead, and Toby wasn't paying the least bit of attention. Instead, he stared out the window with a faraway look on his face while he flipped the buttons on the camera back and forth. Hanna stopped reading. When Toby didn't seem to notice, she cleared her throat. "You don't want me to read to you anymore?"

Her heart melted when a single tear rolled down Toby's cheek. The boy shook his head.

Anxious to find out what troubled the child, she probed a little deeper. "Are you sad, Toby?"

His tiny fingers on the camera stilled. "I don't want to go back to the orphanage." He spoke softly, as if he didn't want anyone else to overhear his biggest secret.

"Oh, I'm sorry." Hanna sighed. She had to find a way to help the child who'd lost his mother in childbirth, his father to the war. "You know what I do when I'm sad?"

Toby's blue eyes scoured her face with an intense gaze. The child was far too intelligent to accept the platitudes and false bravery that fooled so many others. She took a breath. Only one thing had brought her a measure of comfort over the last six months. For Toby's sake, she'd share it.

"I try to help somebody else who's sad."

The boy's thin lips turned down at the corners. "But I'm just a kid. I don't have anybody to help."

"You're helping me," Hanna confessed. She watched as the small child turned the idea over in his head.

"Are you sad, Nurse Hanna?" he asked at last.

Hanna stared at a spot on the wall over the little boy's head. "Sad" was an understatement. Sometimes, she thought she'd drown in her grief. But she'd stopped by to cheer Toby up, not to pull him down into despair with her. Deliberately, she shook aside her own feelings. "Everyone gets sad sometimes, Toby," she pointed out. She summoned a bright smile. "Spending time with you makes me very happy." When a tiny bit of interest flickered in Toby's eyes, she leaned forward. Determined to chase away his blues, she let a teasing note creep into her voice. "I bet you don't know what's coming tonight."

A wide, snaggle-toothed grin spread across Toby's face. "Do, too," he insisted. Ever so carefully, he twisted a button on the camera.

"Oh, yeah? What?" Hanna challenged, although she wouldn't have been at all surprised to learn that Toby knew all about the event that had the whole town buzzing.

"The comet!"

"You are so right!" Hanna patted the child's arm and did her best to hide her concern at his thin frame. Slighter than most boys his age, Toby had lost weight during his stay in the children's ward. Most kids did.

Although the food at the county hospital was good, it didn't compare to home cooking.

"Is the comet a miracle?" Toby's little face scrunched as if he was working hard at solving one of the world's biggest mysteries.

"Hmmm." She nodded while she made a mental note to contact the orphanage. Someone there needed to make sure the boy spent the holidays with a family in town. "That's a good question."

"What's the difference between a miracle and"— he tapped his chin thoughtfully—"and something that just happens? Like, um, rain. Is rain a miracle?"

Hanna studied the child. She'd known all along that Toby was a smart boy, but his questions dug much deeper than what anyone would've expected from a youngster. Beneath the folds of her skirt, she crossed her fingers and wished for a Christmas miracle for Toby. He shouldn't be in the orphanage. He should be in a home with parents who could give him all the attention and encouragement he deserved. "Maybe everything is a miracle." She bent forward to tickle Toby's arm and delighted in his giggle. "Rain. Comets. You. Me. It just depends on how you look at it."

"People are calling this the Christmas Comet, but that's not its real name." Toby straightened against his pillows.

"Is that right?" Interested in this new piece of information, Hanna tilted her head.

"It's the De Vico Comet. That's the person who

discovered it. I read it in a book," he said, rather proud of himself. "And you know what?"

"What?"

"It won't come again until seventy-one years. And you know what else?" The child's eyes widened.

"What?" she asked, enjoying the conversation.

"I know a secret." He crooked a finger on his free hand to beckon her forward.

She leaned in, eager to share the little boy's confidence.

"I think comets are miracles," he said with very adult-like conviction.

"You just might be right about that." She favored the boy with a wide smile, pleased to see that he'd pulled out of his sadness. For a while, they talked of other things—what Toby wanted to be when he grew up, the places he wanted to see, the things he wanted to do. Hanna suppressed her doubts when the child talked of college and the discoveries he'd make. Unless he was adopted, the orphanage would farm him out as day labor in a few years or, if he was very lucky, apprentice him to learn a trade. Even though he was a smart boy, the odds were against him graduating from high school, much less getting a higher education.

"Yoo-hoo!"

While she considered possible ways to change Toby's future for the better, Dottie skipped into the room, all bright smiles and cheery good will.

"Our shift is over, and we've been waiting for you! Hurry. We don't want to be late for the Christmas party." Dottie danced to the side of Toby's bed and bent down. The necklace of tinsel she wore around her neck sparkled as she moved. "Do you mind if I borrow her for a while, Toby?"

Toby flipped another lever on the camera. He pondered the matter for a moment before he gave a solemn nod. "Okay."

Hanna aimed her best smile at the little boy. "I have to go now, Toby. I'll see you tomorrow, but don't forget the comet tonight. I'll be watching for it, too." A warm spot in her chest expanded at the child's broad grin.

"Right!" He snapped his fingers and waved good-bye.

Her heart lighter than it had been when she'd walked into the ward, Hanna hurried to catch up with her friend. The truth of the conversation she'd shared with Toby struck home, and she hugged herself. Helping others really did help push the sadness away, at least for a little while.

In the stairwell, the sounds of the party underway on the floor above drifted down around them. Hanna hesitated, her hand on the rail. Struck by a guilty pang, she cast a lingering look at the door she'd just walked through. How could she leave Toby all alone while she went off and had a good time?

"C'mon! They've started without us." Dottie glanced over her shoulder. Her eagerness to join the rest of the group showed in the excited flush of color that had sprung to her cheeks. She tapped her fingers in impatience.

Hanna gave the doorway a final look. Promising to check in on Toby first thing in the morning, she shoved aside her misgivings and sped up the stairs. Dottie hurried ahead, the rubber soles of her shoes striking the risers in time with the Christmas carol someone played on the old upright piano in the staff break room.

In perfect pitch, a man's strong tenor rang through the stairwell. The volume swelled as others joined in singing a familiar Christmas carol.

"Did you hear that? Dr. Axlerod has such a beautiful voice." Dottie pressed one hand to her heart. "He's like an opera singer. Just listen!"

But not everyone had been blessed with the doctor's gift for music. Hanna winced as someone struck a false note. The owner of a sweet soprano stumbled over the words.

Dottie giggled and clamped a hand over her mouth. "That's Mary Grace," she explained. "She can never remember the lyrics. She's a riot." Practically taking the steps two at a time, she urged, "C'mon!"

At the landing, Dottie darted toward the nurses and doctors who'd gathered around the Christmas tree. Icicles hanging from its branches shimmied as the air currents stirred. Tiny balls of color, reflections from the tree lights, danced against the walls, giving the room a cheerful, rosy glow. Glasses clinked as the festive group toasted one another with apple cider.

Hanna took one look at the party and bit her lower lip. She could do this. She repeated the same message she'd been giving herself throughout the holiday season. She could, but she… she needed a minute. Turning aside, she spied the telephone alcove. Her footsteps slowed. She plucked Dottie's sleeve. "I just want to make a phone call first."

"Now?" On the woman's face, the desire to join the party played tug-of-war with a firm resolve to stick by her friend.

"It's for Toby," she explained, focusing her thoughts on the little boy who sat in a hospital bed without anyone to visit him. She might not be able to change his future, but she could at least see that he had one nice holiday to remember. "I just want to make sure someone from the orphanage takes him home for Christmas."

Compassion darkened Dottie's eyes. "Oh. Poor little boy. Go ahead. Make the call. Then, join us."

"I'll be there in a minute. Promise," Hanna said, relieved. Though she wasn't sure she felt up to joining the party, she didn't want to spoil the fun for her friend.

But Dottie saw through her tricks. "Don't forget. We're *all* going to the gazebo," she warned just as, in the room behind her, Dr. Axlerod launched into a rousing version of "Deck the Halls." Her eyes widened. "That's my favorite." She grinned and dashed into the room.

Slowly, Hanna walked to the phone perched on a

stand in the corner of the hallway. Lifting the receiver to her ear, she spun the heavy rotary dial. When the operator asked who she'd like to call, she responded that she wanted to be put through to the Central Falls Orphanage.

"I'm sorry. That line's out of order," the woman from the phone company explained.

"Thanks," Hanna answered, though her shoulders rounded. "I'll try again later." Hoping the repairs wouldn't take long, she headed back the way she'd come. But at the door to the lounge, she stopped.

Her friends all wanted her to join in the fun. To at least act as if everything was back to normal. She knew they meant well, and she appreciated it. They were only encouraging her to move forward with her life because they loved her and wanted what was best for her. In her heart, she thanked them for their concern. But this year—when so many were celebrating the safe return of loved ones—the holiday cheer and the decorations and the smells of gingerbread fresh from the oven had snuck up on her. And to be quite honest with herself, she wasn't ready. Not for the wassail bowls. Not for the presents with their pretty bows. Not for Christmas carols and songs about hope and peace on earth, goodwill toward men.

Most certainly, her sadness would ruin the party for everyone else, she decided. With a last look at the happy group, she slipped down the stairs and out of sight before anyone could notice.

Alone in the nurses' locker room a short while later,

she exchanged her uniform for the green dress that had been one of Chet's favorites and traded her sturdy white nursing shoes for the pretty red pumps she'd worn because of the holiday. Quickly, she buckled the thin ankle straps. Though the party upstairs might go on for an hour or so, she couldn't take the chance that Dottie or one of the other nurses would catch her while she was still in the hospital.

As she walked out of the main entrance a few minutes later, she glanced up at Toby's room. Like he did every night, the young tyke stood at the window, waiting to wave goodbye to her.

Hanna grinned up at him, and then made a silly face. With a jaunty wave, she headed down the long sidewalk to the parking lot. She'd only gone a yard or two when hurried footsteps sounded behind her. She stepped aside as an orderly hustled past, carrying several cardboard boxes. He'd almost reached the end of the walkway when the young man skidded on an icy spot.

"Whoa!" he cried, juggling the boxes while he recovered his balance.

"Need some help, Charlie?" Hanna hurried to his side, arriving just in time to catch one of the boxes before it hit the ground. Inside the sturdy cardboard, items shifted. Glass tinkled. "I hope nothing broke."

"I think everything's okay." Charlie jostled the box slightly. "It's more Christmas decorations for the gazebo. I'm headed there now so we can get the last of them up before the lighting ceremony tonight. And I'm late."

"Well, be careful. It wouldn't do at all for you to take a spill and break a leg. Or the ornaments—they mean so much to the town." As a child, she'd looked on with wonder during the lighting ceremony. When they were in their teens, she and Chet had helped hang the decorations. As adults, they'd strolled around the gazebo and admired the lights every Christmas Eve.

"Oh, darn it." Charlie's feet skidded the tiniest bit. "I was in such a rush that I forgot to hang up the spare key to the storage locker before I left. You think you could be a doll and take it back inside for me?"

"I wish I could." She wanted to help out. Honest, she did. But turning back now meant she'd probably run into Dottie. Her friend was sure to give her the third degree about skipping the party. She didn't think she could face that tonight. Besides, if anyone absolutely had to get into the locker before morning, they could borrow a key from the head nurse. She had one for every cupboard and closet in the building.

The tips of the orderly's ears pinked as the young man eyed her street clothes. "I'd take it back myself, but I'm leaving first thing in the morning to spend the holiday with my folks." His brow puckered. "Say. No one's gonna need the key tonight. What say you take it home with you and hang it back up in the morning? It would sure help a fella out."

Hanna tilted her head. "I guess I could. As long as no one will need it in the meantime."

"Nah." Charlie crunched a bit of snow under his shoe. "That closet's as empty as my wallet. I got the last of the decorations right here." He tapped his fingers against the side of a box. "If you wouldn't mind, the key's right here in my jacket pocket." Turning, he leaned down to bring his shoulder within arm's reach.

Feeling just a touch self-conscious, she fished out the key. Hastily, she tucked it into her coat pocket, where she was sure to remember it when she arrived at work the next day.

"Thanks, Nurse Hanna. You're a peach." Charlie righted the boxes in his arms. He hurried off in the direction of the town center.

"Careful!" Hanna called after him. She gave the key in her pocket a final pat before, heeding her own warning, she picked her slow and cautious way toward the parking lot.

By the time she reached her car, fat snowflakes covered the sidewalk in a fresh blanket of white. She sniffled, just a little, as she brushed the icy mix from the windshield of the 1943 Hudson. Chet had driven the car straight from the showroom to their house the week before he'd shipped out. He'd always taken such good care of her. She'd so looked forward to doing the same for him and spending the rest of her life making a home for him. With Chet's degree in Civil Engineering, he'd go to work building houses or schools after the war ended. There'd be babies, of course. Once they came along, she'd quit her job at the hospital. Instead, she'd spend her days keeping house, raising their children, and helping out in the community. They'd have a good life, one filled with baseball games and dance recitals, PTA meetings and the Women's League, dinners with important clients and family vacations. Or, at least, that was the future they'd dreamed of. Without Chet, none of those plans meant anything anymore, so, with a sigh, she slipped behind the wheel.

A few minutes later, she slowed as she passed the gazebo where, despite the impending storm, a crowd gathered. Beneath the pitched roof, Charlie pulled several ornaments from one of the boxes. The colorful balls no sooner dangled from his fingers than two girls about his age rushed to his side. Hanna smiled to herself. No wonder the young man had been in such a hurry to get to the gazebo.

Drawing in a steadying breath, she pressed lightly on the gas. She hoped Dottie and their friends would understand if she didn't show up at the lighting ceremony tonight. For now, she just wanted to go home and be alone with her memories.

A short time later, she steered the car onto the driveway that ran beside a tidy little house on a tree-lined street. Already, snow blanketed the sidewalks and walkways. It piled up along the curbs. She stomped the wintery mix from her shoes on the mat by the front door. Stepping into the house, she let down her guard as she hung her coat and hat on the coat tree by the door. Within these walls, she didn't need to keep a stiff upper lip or pretend that she was over the pain of losing Chet. Here, in the home they'd barely begun to furnish before he'd left, she could be herself.

She fixed herself a cup of tea and settled into the chair by the window. On the other side of the panes, the snow fell thicker. It muffled the sounds of the occasional car on her street. A deep and mournful howl came from somewhere nearby. She brushed the dampness from her cheeks and peered through the glass, but the only movement came from the steam that rose in thin tendrils from her cup on the end table. She took a sip. Over the rim of the china, she eyed the decorations she'd put out in hopes of creating a festive air in the house that was too big, too quiet, for one person. She'd bought the smallest Christmas tree they'd had on the lot this year. It stood, slightly canted to one side, in the corner. Money had been tight, and she hadn't had any to spare for lights, but she'd strung a garland of cranberries and popcorn across the tree's branches. She'd even spent an entire evening cutting strips of newspaper and pasting the links together in a long chain that she'd draped from the green limbs. Though she wished there were more gifts under the tree, she'd lovingly wrapped each one and tied them off with bright red bows. She smiled, thinking how Toby's face would light up when he opened his on Christmas morning. Would he like the books she'd chosen for him?

After fortifying herself with another sip of tea, she

pulled a leather-bound album onto her lap. Paging through it, she lingered over favorite pictures where Chet's face smiled up at her. She couldn't help but smile in return as she recalled the happy moments of their time together. She traced one finger over a picture of Chet as a boy. He leaned against a fencepost, grinning, his hands in the pockets of his overalls as if he hadn't just tugged on her pigtails and ran away before she could catch him. She turned the page and studied a more recent photo. She'd snapped this one at the train station when Chet had gotten a three-day pass just before he'd shipped out. He'd looked so handsome stepping from the train, all dark good looks and swagger, in his uniform. His confidence that they'd win the war had been infectious, and she'd been caught up in his certainty that he'd come home to her. But it hadn't turned out that way, and, long before she wanted to, she reached the last page in the album.

Outside, a dog barked. This time, a frantic pawing at her front door accompanied a fearful whining.

"Oh, my goodness." She closed the photo album and set it aside.

The moment she opened the door, a golden retriever burst into the room. Little more than a puppy, the dog gave a happy sound and shook, spattering the bare hardwood with clumps of ice and snow.

"Oh! Poor baby. Are you cold?" A laugh bubbled in her throat, and she stopped herself. Of course the dog was cold. With the snow coming down by the bucketful, he was lucky he hadn't frozen to death.

Who knew how long he'd been stuck out there? She rushed down the hall, grabbed a towel and a blanket from the closet, and raced back to his side.

"This'll get you warmed up." She treated the dog to a vigorous rubdown. As she worked, golden strands of thick fur sifted through her fingers. When she heard a metallic clink from the collar around his neck, she breathed a sigh of relief. The pretty puppy wasn't a stray. He had owners. People who must miss him terribly. She kneeled beside the pup and felt for his tags. "Ruffin," she read out loud. "Is that your name?"

In answer to her question, Ruffin licked her hand.

"Good dog," she said, giving him a big hug. "Are you lost, Ruffin? You're a ways from home, aren't you?" According to his tags, the dog belonged to a family who lived off Main Street, not far from the gazebo. She glanced out the window. Snow fell steadily. If this kept up, the streets would soon be impassible. Grabbing a pencil and a slip of paper, she copied the information from Ruffin's tag. "Okay, boy. I'm going to call your folks and let them know where you are."

As if he understood, the dog wagged his tail. With a heavy sigh, he flopped down on the floor near the heater.

Hanna shook her head. The young pup had to be exhausted after his ordeal. Leaving him to his nap, she headed for the phone. Her stomach sank before she even held the receiver to her ear. Other people were using the party line she shared with the rest of the neighbors on her street.

"… and her tone of voice," one woman said. "Let me tell you. Miss Know-It-All!"

Filled with self-importance, a different voice replied, "It's just a phase. Tina did the same thing."

"Excuse me," Hanna interrupted as politely as she could. "I'd like to make a call."

"—week? We were listening to the radio—"

Frustrated when the conversation between the women continued as if she hadn't spoken, Hanna raised her voice. "Excuse me. I'd like to make a call."

"Uh!" The first speaker made an irritated sound. "Is this an emergency?" she demanded.

"Well, no…" Not technically, it wasn't. If she couldn't make a call, no one would die or anything. She studied the snow that fell beyond her window. "But I—"

"If it's not an *emergency*, you'll have to wait your turn," Miss Snippy said.

As if trying to make up for her friend's rudeness, the other voice broke in. "We'll be off in a jiff."

"Right." Figuring the odds of that happening were about the same as the sun bursting through the storm clouds in the night sky, Hanna hesitated. She'd pay a big fine or even get arrested if she claimed she needed the phone for an emergency when she didn't. Even if it had been, she couldn't force the women to get off the line. With no choice in the matter, she lowered the receiver into its cradle. She glanced at the dog. "Well, Ruffin. What do we do now?"

In answer, he scurried across the floor to the door. Whining, he sniffed at it.

"Oh, I know." She patted the dog's thick fur. "I tried."

Not at all satisfied, Ruffin lifted one paw and placed it in her lap. The dog's pleading whimpers cut straight through her heart. Was someone missing their pet as much as he missed his owners? The collar of her dress felt tight around her neck. She tugged at the wool and cleared her throat. She'd do her part to get the pup home to the people who loved him. It was the least she could do.

Taking her coat from its hook by the door, she leaned down. "Want to go home, Ruffin? Do you, boy?"

With an eager look, the retriever issued a happy bark.

"I'll take that as a yes." She grabbed her purse and keys.

A treacherous twenty minutes later, she eased onto a driveway beside a two-story home trimmed with garlands of green and strands of multi-colored lights. When she tapped the horn to announce her arrival, the front door sprang open almost immediately. Warm, inviting light spilled from the house as a woman stepped out onto the spacious porch. Seeing her, Ruffin leaped toward the windshield. His paws on the dashboard, he barked excitedly.

"Recognize someone, do you, boy?" Hanna asked. She held the car door wide.

"Ruffin?" The woman on the porch took several steps forward. Beneath fashionable dark curls, shock and disbelief played across her finely chiseled features. "Oh, my gosh. Hal, it's Ruffin," she called over her shoulder.

As soon as Hanna opened the car door, Ruffin bounded from the front seat. Taking the steps three at a time, as only a young dog could, he leaped to the spot where a woman not much older than Hanna herself kneeled. Happy tears streamed down the young owner's face as she wrapped her arms around the dog's neck.

"I guess it goes without saying that he's yours," Hanna said, smiling at the antics of the excited puppy. "I'm Hanna Morse. Ruffin knocked on my door tonight, pretty as you please, and asked me if I wouldn't mind bringing him home to you."

"I can't thank you enough." The owner buried her face in the dog's fur for a long moment. With a start, she jumped to her feet. "Oh! Where are my manners? I'm Sue Bunce. Please, please come in." Sue opened the door behind her and stifled a giggle as Ruffin darted past. "Come here, Ruffin. Come here," she ordered, but the boisterous dog kept on going.

"Only for a minute," Hanna murmured. It'd be good to get warm before she started the long drive home. But she wouldn't stay. Not with the snow falling in thick clumps and the roads getting sloppier by the minute.

Following Sue, she stepped into a parlor where a dozen or more Christmas cards lined a mantel edged with swags of greenery. The inviting scent of gingerbread mingled with the smoke that rose from the wood stove and bathed the house in the warm smells of the season. Sue didn't stand on ceremony but immediately sank to her knees on the carpet. As if she didn't trust her eyes, she buried her hands in the dog's fur.

"This is my husband, Hal," she announced, nodding to the snappily dressed man who trotted down the stairs. "Oh, Hal! Isn't it wonderful? Hanna brought Ruffin home to us!" She hugged the dog to her. Cupping the pup's face in her hands, she asked, "Where were you, you bad boy. Hmmm? Where have you been?"

Hal's eyes crinkled and the corners of his mouth lifted. "She lives for that dog," he said, though his own love for their pet was as plain as the smile on his face.

"Honestly, I never knew how much until just now," Sue agreed. She laughed when the dog pushed closer. His tail wagged furiously, as if he wanted his owners to know he'd never run away again. "Right, boy?" Tears glistened in the dark eyes she aimed at Hanna. "Gosh. I don't know what we would have done if you hadn't brought him home. You're our hero."

"Oh, no." Hanna dismissed that idea out of hand. "Heroes change the world. I just did a simple thing."

Sue scrambled to her feet. "Well, you saved our Christmas, I can tell you that. Can you imagine how broken-hearted we would all be if we had to spend Christmas without Ruffin?"

Hanna's breath stalled in her chest. She knew

all too well how difficult it was to spend Christmas missing someone you loved. She edged toward the door. "I should be going," she managed.

"Are you sure?" Sue crossed to the window, where she pulled the heavy drape aside. "Hanna, it's getting really bad out there. Why don't you spend the night here?"

How sweet.

She gave the invitation a moment's thought as she looked about the room. Short laces tied in a pretty bow, a pair of white baby shoes glowed among the twinkling lights on the Christmas tree. The comfy, red leather chair by the wood stove probably belonged to Mr. Bunce, while the Queen Anne's chair beyond it was most likely the spot Sue preferred. A basket of chew toys stood beside a cozy dog's bed in one corner. Hanna swallowed hard. This, she said to herself, this was the kind of home she'd hoped to make for her and Chet.

"I couldn't. Really." Putting her best effort into maintaining her smile, she backed toward the door.

A baby's thin wail floated down the stairs.

"Oh, that's little Clara." Sue's face fell. "I didn't have the heart to tell her that Ruffin was missing."

"I'll go up and tuck her in." Before anyone could argue, Hal headed for the stairs. "I can give her the good news about her puppy."

Sue took another quick peek out the window. "Won't you please stay the night? The snow is really coming down."

"Thanks for the offer, but I don't live far. Just over on Elm Street." Hanna pulled on her gloves. With a young child, as well as an active dog to take care of, Sue needed an overnight guest as much as they all needed another snow storm.

"Are you sure there's no way we can thank you?" Sue trailed her to the door.

"You already have." Knowing that Ruffin would share the holiday with his family was thanks enough. "Merry Christmas."

"You, too. Drive safe." One hand clutching Ruffin by the collar, Sue waved goodbye.

"I will," Hanna promised as she let herself out.

On the front porch, she sucked in a surprised gasp. During the short time she'd spent inside, the storm had transformed the landscape into a winter wonderland. Tall trees bent under the weight of the falling snow. A thick layer of white made it difficult to see where the driveway ended and the street began. Overhead, cloud cover obscured the stars.

"Oh!" With the storm raging, Toby wouldn't get to see the De Vico Comet tonight after all. She hoped her favorite patient wouldn't be too disappointed.

She hesitated for another second, wondering if she'd made a huge mistake by turning down Sue's hospitality. But the thought of spending the night with the Bunces, of watching the family enjoy the life she'd dreamed of sharing with Chet, was too much, so, steeling herself against the cold, she headed for her car.

With several inches of snow on the ground, getting

out of the driveway presented a challenge, but she overcame it. Creeping along well below her normal speed, she half expected conditions to improve once she reached the center of town. But a gust of gut-tightening wind buffeted the car as she turned onto Main Street. The wiper blades lost ground against the mix of snow and ice that fell harder and thicker with every passing moment. She urged the blades to swish back and forth faster. Her breath fogged the windows, reducing her view of the world beyond the glass to two small half circles. Thunder rolled above her. Her grip on the steering wheel tightened until her hands ached.

Even though it meant she didn't have to worry about traffic, the fact that hers was the only car on the road made her heart race. Forcing herself to stay calm, she overruled the little voice in her head that goaded her to drive faster, *faster*. Instead, she eased her foot from the gas pedal until the big Hudson moved at a snail's pace. Still, that wasn't enough. Her breath froze in her chest as the tires skidded across an icy patch. The car shimmied. The steering wheel slid beneath her fingers. She grabbed for it and held on tight, but the big car only spun in a lazy circle. It landed with a metal-rending thump in a snow drift. The engine ticked.

Hanna shuddered out a breath. She flexed her fingers, wiggled her feet. Nothing hurt. She hadn't been injured; she had that much to be thankful for.

She goosed the gas. A loud whine came from the rear of the car. The tires spun in useless circles on the ice.

With a groan, she shifted into reverse and, offering up a little prayer, pressed on the gas. The car didn't budge.

She drummed her fingers on the steering wheel. Sitting here wasn't the answer. Long before morning, she'd run out of gas. Without gas, the heater that barely kept the cold at bay would quit altogether. If that happened, she'd freeze to death while the blizzard howled around her. Much as she'd rather stay put, she needed to get someplace warm and dry.

A deep pile of snow blocked her door. Unable to open it, she slid across the front seat, forced the passenger side door open, and climbed out into the drift. Ice spilled over the tops of her shoes and melted onto her hose. She shivered as the harsh wind whipped her hair. Clamping a hand on her hat, she struggled through the snow bank to an area where the wet powder lay only a foot or so deep. With everything covered in a thickening blanket of white, nothing looked familiar. Though she couldn't identify any landmarks, she knew she had to be near the center of town. In the distance, a halo of light broke through the darkness.

That has to be the gazebo. If she could just make it that far, she'd be all right. Though the swirling snow made it hard to see, she trusted that there'd be people on the square, people who could help her. Not more than an hour earlier, she'd seen the gathering crowd. Surely, they'd still be there singing carols and drinking hot chocolate. She only had to make it that far to find help. To find warmth.

The blinding snow made even a short walk heavy, treacherous going. Her head down, she cautiously studied every step. Bit by bit, she forged a path. Ice crunched beneath her shoes. Her leather soles skidded. The punishing wind tugged and pried at every opening, every seam in her coat. Wet, cold droplets pelted her brow, clung to her hair, and sent chills down her back.

She pressed on, determined.

Her foot struck a wooden step, and her head jerked up. After what had seemed like an eternity of trudging through the snow, she'd finally reached the gazebo. She turned in a slow circle without seeing another soul. Doubt landed a solid punch to her stomach.

Had she come all this way for nothing?

She wasted no time in taking stock. What was the use? Her fingers had already grown so numb she'd had trouble looping her purse over her arm. The cold seared her lungs with every breath. Her feet had turned into blocks of ice. If she didn't find shelter soon, she'd be frozen stiff by morning.

Through the clouds, an odd light lit the sky. She squinted in the dim glow and spotted a storage barn she'd never noticed before. It stood not more than fifty yards from her. Could she make it that far? She had to. Pulling her coat as tightly about her as she could, she set off, determined, if nothing else, to get out of the wind, out of the snow.

Ominous thunder rolled overhead. Lightning flashed in the distance. The sky grew brighter. A faint glow cast an eerie light on the snow. A shiver ran straight down her spine. By sheer force of will, she made her feet move faster.

It took every ounce of strength she had left, and then some, to reach the barn. Wrenching the door open, she stepped inside. She barely had time to shut herself in before, trembling with exhaustion, her legs gave out. She sank to her knees. Just as she did, a sudden burst of lightning clapped the building. The air pulsed with such force, it flung her across the tiny space. Blinding pain seared through her as her head struck something hard and unforgiving.

And everything went dark.

Chapter Three

December 2016

Parked outside the Central Falls Police Headquarters, Jake Stanton scanned the freshly
shoveled sidewalks for signs of trouble and got…
nothing. Stifling a ripple of discontent, he brushed
a drop of melted snow from the sleeve of his uniform
jacket. Where had this feeling of dissatisfaction come
from? Christmas was right around the corner. The
sights and sounds of his favorite season had always
filled him with anticipation and hope. Not so this
year. This year, the holiday greetings of people he'd
known all his life left him feeling empty and hollow.
Not even a drive down Main Street, where Christmas
lights shone around every doorway and window, could
brighten his spirits.

He tapped his chin. He supposed the blame for
his current case of the blues fell squarely on his own

shoulders. But who could fault him for feeling down when his number one goal was to help people, to make a difference in their lives… and no one needed his assistance? From Mr. Birchdale at the Art Gallery to Tobias Cook, the town's somewhat eccentric millionaire, everyone in Central Falls had their lives tied up in neat packages, much like the Christmas present that busybody, Mrs. Jones, had just toted out of the china shop.

Not that he wanted to change professions. No. He'd dreamed of becoming a police officer ever since he'd pinned a shiny tin badge on his shirt and strapped a toy gun in a holster around his waist at three years old. He'd pursued that goal by signing up for the military police when he'd enlisted in the Army straight out of high school. Four years as an MP, followed by another four in college, had earned him a position with the police department in his hometown. For the past five years, he'd risen steadily through the ranks. Last fall, he'd been promoted to Training Officer, a position he'd thoroughly enjoyed until three months ago… when Sarah had joined the force.

He guessed *she* was the other part of his problem. As Training Officer, it had fallen to him to teach her the ins and outs of good police work—to slow down, to assess every situation, to stay safe. A tough enough job with any new recruit. But working with Sarah made that task twice as hard. In order to do his job right, he had to stop seeing her as the little tomboy who'd done her best to outrun, outshoot, outmaneuver him all through their childhood. He had to look at her through fresh eyes. And well, that was nearly impossible when she insisted on treating him the same way she always had. Take right now, for example.

"What's your favorite?" Sarah posed the question from behind the steering wheel of their squad car.

Jake started. What had she been talking about? Oh, yeah. Sports. "Football. Definitely football."

"Over baseball?" Sarah's blond brows rose to incredulous points. Her lips formed a thin line, and she gave her head a shake that sent her long ponytail swaying. "You do not."

"What? You think you know everything about me?" He swirled the coffee in his Styrofoam cup.

"Yeah, I kinda do." Sarah shrugged. "I've known you your whole life."

"Okay, you do not know everything there is to know about me." She might think she understood what drove him, but how could she? He'd never once mentioned how much he wanted to make a difference, to do something worthwhile with his life. There were other things she didn't know about him, too. For instance, he'd certainly never confessed how much he worried about her when they went out on a call.

Giving her his best smug smile, the one she never saw through, he eyed her over the rim of his cup. "A man needs to keep some things to himself."

"Oh, so you're a *man of mystery* now." She laughed. "Not!"

"You'll see." Folding his arms across his chest, he

kept his secrets to himself. With her quick wit and keen intelligence, his partner would make a fine police officer one day. Once she started taking him seriously, that was.

Her expression said she had him all figured out as she squared around to face him. "Besides, Louise tells me anything I want to know."

Louise never could keep a secret.

"Oh, please, shoot me now. Why?" Jake leaned back against the headrest. The long-suffering sigh he'd practiced until he had it down pat eased through his lips. "Why am I partners with my little sister's best friend?"

"'Cause you trust me?" Reaching across the squad car, Sarah tapped her fist against his chest.

An unexpected urge to catch her fingers in his stirred within him. He suppressed it and batted her hand away. "Ma'am, hands on your side of the vehicle," he said, the warning as much a reminder to himself as it was for her.

"And I"—Sarah gave his arm another tap—"make you look good."

As if! Jake chuckled. "Could you please be a little less bratty when you're in uniform?"

Sarah tilted her head. Her Cheshire-cat grin offered no promises.

A burst of static rose from the radio mounted under the dash. "Dispatch to 403."

Jake keyed the mic attached to his uniform collar. "Yeah, 403 here."

"We have a report of a female on Main Street at Center Road who may need a well-being check. Can you investigate that?"

"Copy that. En route." He wasted a glance at Sarah, but she'd already moved into action, buckling her seatbelt and stashing her coffee in a cup holder in the smooth, measured movements he'd drilled into her over the past three months. The throaty engine of the 4x4 that could handle even the worst road conditions rumbled as she put the SUV in gear.

In the seat beside her, Jake straightened and peered through the windshield. Maybe this would be it. Maybe this would be the call that gave him a chance to make a difference in Central Falls and restored his Christmas spirit. Moments later, he searched for anything out of place among the happy shoppers who ambled along Main Street. The Jones boy—George, he recalled—leaned against a light pole, his phone pressed against his ear. Nothing unusual there. A pair of boys on skateboards rolled past the squad car. Jake dismissed them. As long as they wore helmets and pads and didn't mistake Main Street for a race track, the town's young folk were welcome on the city sidewalks. His focus shifted to a pair of women who faced one another on the other side of the wide thoroughfare. An odd feeling prickled the back of his neck when one of the pair moved farther down the street, a guide dog's harness in one hand, a white cane in the other. His attention zeroed in on the woman who remained behind.

"There." He pointed to a young blonde who wore an unfashionable gray coat.

"Her?" Though doubt filled her tone, Sarah pulled to the curb.

"Yeah, the one wringing her hands." Trusting Sarah to guard his back, Jake stepped from their squad car as soon as the tires stopped rolling. He moved lightly over the packed snow. Braced for action, he positioned himself in front of the slight figure on the sidewalk, shielding his less-experienced partner with his body in case the stranger made any sudden moves. He pitched his voice to catch her attention. "Excuse me, miss."

He'd always been a detail man. His military training and his time on the force here in Central Falls had helped solidify his focus. Now, he catalogued images. The agitated woman wore a tiny pillbox hat that looked more decorative than functional. Her wool coat appeared to be well-enough made, but it wouldn't keep her warm if she stayed outside for long. A pair of thin, leather gloves offered scant protection against freezing temperatures. Her shoes—with their heels and decorative stitching—hadn't been made for traipsing around in the snow, either. His gaze bounced to a wrinkled brow and brightly painted, pursed lips.

Instinct told him she didn't pose a danger. The look he traded with Sarah assured him that his partner was of the same mind, and he dialed his tension down a bit.

"Is everything okay?" he asked the woman.

"I—" Tears welled in her blue eyes. "Can you help me?"

"That's what we're here for, ma'am." He took the lead while Sarah whipped a notebook out of her pocket and began taking notes. "What seems to be the problem?"

"Well, I… I had an accident last night." She worried her lower lip with even white teeth. "My car got stuck in a snowdrift. I made it to a barn, but then I, I passed out or something. When I woke up, everything was… different." Slowly, she stared at the police car at the curb as if she'd never seen one like it. "And I don't know how to get back home. Can you help me?"

"You say you were in an accident?" Jake gave the woman an appraising look. Her clothing, though odd, seemed to be intact. She had no obvious injuries.

"Yes…" Her soft voice faded. "I made it as far as the gazebo." She took a step toward the street. "I just, I just need to find my car. And my purse. I think I left it in the barn."

"Whoa, now!" Jake grasped the woman by the arm. In her current state, she could walk into traffic and get hurt. "I think the first thing we ought to do is get you checked out. Make sure you haven't bumped your head or something. Then, we'll have a look around for that car. Let's let my partner here get some information. Okay?"

"Name," Sarah asked, focused on her notebook.

"Hanna. Hanna Morse. I live at 166 Elm Street."

Giving Sarah a puzzled look, she asked, "When did Central Falls hire a woman police officer?"

"I've been on the force three months, ma'am." Turning far enough to one side that Hanna couldn't see, Sarah rolled her eyes. Her words aimed for his ears only, she added, "Elm Street's in the business district. Pretty sure the Organic Planet is at 166."

Jake nodded and keyed his mic. "Dispatch. Tell Chief Munson we're en route to Doc Lipscomb's with one Hanna Morse. Ask him to meet us there." Whatever was wrong with the woman they'd found, Jake had a feeling they'd need Chief Munson's help in getting to the bottom of it.

Twenty minutes later, Jake motioned Sarah to her feet as the chief stood when Dr. Jessica Lipsomb entered the waiting area of the small clinic. "Hanna Morse appears to be healthy," she announced to a trio of relieved smiles. "She has no obvious signs of a concussion. Her vision is fine. She has no headaches. I know you're eager to ask her some questions. She agreed to talk with you while we finish up here."

Dr. Lipscomb beckoned the three of them to join her in the exam room. There, she took a blood pressure cuff from a rack on the wall. Aiming a reassuring smile at the patient seated on the exam table, she wrapped the device around Hanna's arm. For the next few minutes, the doctor alternated several routine tests with questions that Jake thanked his lucky stars she'd never had to ask him.

"How long do you think you were unconscious?" Dr. Lipscomb placed the cuff back in its holder.

"I don't know." Hanna shook her head. "I, um, I heard a big *boom*. It was thunder, during the storm."

Jake studied the slender blonde. "The storm?"

Beside him, Sarah gave her notepad an attention-getting *tap-tap-tap* and said, "There was no storm last night." She challenged Hanna with a firm look. "Weather was clear as a bell."

"What? No!" Hanna protested. "It was terrible. The thunder and the lightning. There was a strange glow in the sky. After that, though, I must have fallen asleep because that's all I remember." She peered up at them. "Do you think I'm dreaming? You all seem so real, but everything—it, it doesn't seem right."

Chief Munson leaned forward to ask, "How long were you in the shed before you came out?"

"Just the night," Hanna answered immediately. "My car got stuck in the snow."

"Her vital signs are normal," Dr. Lipscomb announced over one shoulder. She held her pen in front of Hanna's face and moved it slowly to one side.

Ignoring the doctor, Hanna rambled on about dreams. "I was reading *Ladies' Home Journal* once, and they had a story on dreams, how they seem real, but…"

"*Shhhh*," Dr. Lipscomb hushed her patient. "Just follow the light with your eyes."

A burst of static sounded in Jake's ear. He pressed his earbud and listened as reports filtered in from his fellow police officers. So far, no one on the force had spotted an abandoned vehicle anywhere within the city limits. The minute Dr. Lipscomb finished testing Hanna's vision, Jake updated Chief Munson on the search.

"Maybe we're looking for the wrong vehicle," the chief suggested. He shifted his focus to the confused young woman. "Can you tell me the make and model?"

Jake studied the perplexed frown that crossed Hanna's features. He wasn't at all surprised when she asked, "Of what?"

"Of your car," the chief said in the patient voice that earned him the respect of staff and suspects alike. "What kind of car do you have?"

"A Hudson. It's a Hudson."

"A what?" Sarah blurted.

Jake smiled to himself. He knew exactly what a Hudson was. There'd been a time when he'd have given his eyeteeth for one of the classic cars.

"My husband bought it right before the war," Hanna offered.

Chief Munson traded a glance with Jake. Now they were getting somewhere. "And has he been contacted?" the chief asked. "Your husband?"

Jake's chest squeezed at the look of incredible sadness that crossed Hanna's face.

"No." Her voice dropped to a whisper. "He died. In the war."

"I'm sorry to hear that," the chief said, while

silence filled the room. "Was he deployed in Iraq? Or Afghanistan?"

The perplexed look that Jake was starting to recognize swam through Hanna's eyes. "He was in Malmedy," she said with a sad sigh.

Jake fought an urge to scratch his head. If he remembered his high school history lessons correctly, Malmedy was the site of the worst POW massacre... of World War II. A single glance at Dr. Lipscomb put any doubt of the matter to rest. And no wonder, considering the Medal of Honor on display in her office. Her grandfather had fought and died in the Battle of the Bulge.

The doctor smoothed one hand down the front of her lab coat. "Mrs. Morse," she said before the chief had a chance to ask his next question, "what's today's date?"

"December 16th." The petite blonde hesitated. "No. The 17th. December 17th," she said, growing more sure of herself.

"And where are we?" the doctor asked as if she wasn't trying to poke holes in Hanna's story. "What city?"

Hanna's pert features brightened. She knew the answer to this one. "Why, in Central Falls, of course."

"And the name of the president?"

Certainty glowed in Hanna's eyes. "Harry S. Truman."

Though Jake's mouth wanted to drop open, he kept it closed. Dr. Lipscomb handed the conversation back to his boss with a single nod.

"Hmm." Chief Munson tapped his foot against the hardwood floor. "Hanna, Dr. Lipscomb… if you don't mind staying right where you are, I'd like to confer with my officers for a moment." Without waiting for a response, the chief headed for the nearest exit, Sarah right on his heels. Bringing up the rear, Jake aimed a sympathetic glance at the woman who looked pretty normal despite her bizarre answers to Dr. Lipscomb's questions.

"Okay," Chief Munson began once the door snapped shut behind them. "What are we dealing with?"

"Amnesia?" Sarah ventured.

"Can't be. She knows her name. City. Date," the chief replied, ticking items off a list. "Though, I'll admit, she's confused about the year."

"Yeah, and there was no storm last night." Sarah rotated her cap in her hands. "Maybe she's pulling a scam?"

"That's possible," the chief agreed. "Her address doesn't check out. Her car doesn't check out."

"Whatever a Hudson is," Sarah added. "She has no ID."

Jake's eyes narrowed. He got where the chief was coming from. Protecting the citizens of Central Falls from harm had to be their boss's primary mission. As for Sarah, she was the newest officer on the force and looking for her first big case to crack. That didn't mean either of them were on the right track. Stepping in before an innocent woman got labeled, he provided a simple reminder. "She says she dropped her purse back in the shed."

"That's a likely story." One that, by the expression on her face, Sarah wasn't buying.

The chief drew in a deep breath. "We're going to have to take her in."

"On what charge?" Jake demanded. It didn't seem fair for the woman to end up on the wrong side of the deal just because she had a few problems with her memory.

"For now, we'll just get more information from her," the chief said, though his brow furrowed at the suggestion.

"It's either that or a 1701," Sarah said, citing the code for involuntary commitment.

"Wait. Hold on, Chief. This all seems a little bit harsh." An odd sensation stirred in Jake's chest. If there'd ever been someone who needed his help, Hanna was it.

Chief Munson held out empty hands as if he wished someone would fill them with a different solution. "It's procedure, Jake. Nothing else."

Jake thought fast. Some sixth sense told him that Hanna would never find herself again if they locked her behind bars or, worse, put her in a psych ward. Though he wasn't buying her story about a husband who died in World War II, he was pretty sure she'd suffered some kind of mental trauma. She needed a place to sit for a while and collect her thoughts more than she needed anything else. Some place where no one bombarded her with questions or forced her to give answers that didn't make any sense. And he knew just such a place.

He cleared his throat. "Let me take her back to the farm, okay? Just for a day or two. Just let her calm down. Let her feel safe."

A rare instance of indecision flickered in the chief's dark eyes. "I don't know," he responded while he tugged at his gloves. "It's against protocol, and I'm not sure she isn't—"

Afraid the next words out of his boss's mouth would condemn Hanna to spending the holidays behind bars, Jake forced himself to ignore the accusations in Sarah's wide-eyed stare. Speaking with far more assurance than he felt, he pleaded Hanna's case. "We haven't processed her yet. Just… let me observe her. If she's delusional, I'll take her to the hospital. If I sense she's a fraud, I'll bring her back to the station."

Chief Munson shook his head. "If she's a con artist, she's going to play you at every turn," he warned.

"C'mon. It's almost Christmas." The thought of anyone needlessly spending the holidays in jail or a hospital ward soured Jake's stomach. Aware that he was crawling out on a very thin limb, he added, "I'll take full responsibility. Okay?"

Two pairs of skeptical eyes stared back at him, but he stood his ground. As far as he knew—and he had a pretty good grasp of the law—living in the past wasn't a crime. And no one, especially not a sad and confused young woman, should have to spend Christmas behind bars for that.

Hanna climbed into the unfamiliar vehicle and clasped her hands in her lap. She took a deep breath. When the officer with the compassionate brown eyes had offered her the choice of spending the night with his family or spending the next few days locked in a cell or in the mental ward of the hospital, well, really there hadn't been much of a choice, had there? But agreeing to go off with a perfect stranger—even a police officer—was one thing. Actually getting into his strange vehicle and letting him take her who-knew-where was something else again. Her head pounded. She closed her eyes and ordered herself to be brave.

"Seat belt," Officer Stanton said, sliding behind the wheel.

She flinched. "What? I'm not wearing a belt." She eyed the dash that looked more like pictures she'd seen of an airplane cockpit than any car she'd ever been in. Of course, she'd never been in a police car before. Maybe they all came equipped with the odd-looking buttons and dials. She bit her lower lip and admitted she wasn't being completely honest with herself, but the alternative was...

She stopped. Whatever the alternative was, she didn't want to consider it.

"You'll have to fasten your seat belt," the police

officer repeated. He tugged on a thick strap that magically lengthened to cross his lap. With a snap, he slid a metal buckle into place.

Hanna took a breath to steady her nerves. She could do this. It was new and different, but she could manage. She fumbled for the strap on her side and gave it a good tug. It slipped out of her fingers. She tried again. This time, she stretched the thick webbing far enough to reach the buckle. But no matter how many times she stabbed the ends together, they wouldn't catch.

"Here, let me help." As if he'd been doing it all his life, the officer snaked the belt across her. "I'm Jake, by the way," he said once the pieces clicked into place.

"Hanna." With one hand, she pulled the strap away from her body. Like a rubber band, it snapped into place again the moment she let go. "Do all police cars have these?" she asked, thinking out loud. "If I'd had one in my car last night, maybe I wouldn't be having this dream right now."

"This must all be very confusing for you." Jake put the car in gear. "For now, why don't you look around while we head through town? Maybe you'll see something that'll jog your memory." His attention on the road ahead, the deputy headed down Main Street.

She supposed she should take his advice. Though what was the point, if this was all make-believe? She rubbed her eyes and stared out the window. Halfway down the block, Jake glided to a stop to let two young boys scoot across the street in front of their car. The kids rode on thin boards, and she had to look twice before she noticed the wheels underneath. How interesting.

Hanna snapped her fingers. That was it! She had to be dreaming about the future, hadn't she? That would explain the sleek-looking cars, the puffy coats everyone wore, the women who paraded about town in slacks and dungarees. Her certainty grew as they passed the square, where the heart of Central Falls had fallen into ruin, seemingly overnight.

"It's too bad you don't decorate the gazebo anymore," she murmured. "It's so pretty with all the lights and decorations. I don't guess you sing carols and drink hot chocolate there, either. Do you?"

"At that eyesore?" Jake spared the run-down fixture in the park a quick look. "No one's paid any attention to that old place in years."

That settled it. This all had to be a dream. That had to be the explanation. Otherwise, she'd have to accept that she'd somehow stepped into the future, and if she admitted that, Jake wouldn't have to lock her in the loony bin. She'd go there voluntarily.

When they reached the edge of town, she leaned back and closed her eyes. *Maybe if I go to sleep, the dream will be over when I wake up.*

But she must not have slept because she roused when the car stopped, and nothing had changed. Jake still wore his puffy blue coat, the police cruiser still had all its strange dials, and a seat belt still strapped her into the vehicle. Fighting tears, she mimicked the officer's motions when he pushed his latch. Her odd belt slithered into its holder. She brushed at her eyes and stared out the window. An enormous barn stood on a snowy hillside. In the distance, she spotted twin silos. Behind her, a rambling house with yellow siding had been decorated for the holidays.

"Oh! I know this place," she exclaimed, taking in the familiar surroundings. "That barn. This house. I've been here before." Eager to prove her point, she sprang from the car and headed for the breezeway that led to the front porch. Her heels rang out on the wooden steps. Breathing a happy sigh, she trailed her fingers through the garland that decorated the white railing for every holiday. A sense of finally arriving home settled into her chest when she recognized the door knocker that peeked out from the center of an evergreen wreath.

"My parents live here in the big house," Jake said, climbing the steps onto the porch behind her. "I live in one of the outbuildings. My sister moved back with her daughter, temporarily."

"Oh, so your parents are the Morgans?" Hanna pointed toward the tall red barn where the livestock spent the winters. "We buy our milk here. The Morgans have the best cows, don't you think?"

"Actually, um…"

She froze when Jake braced his hands on his hips. He shook his head, and her breath stalled in her chest. Whatever came next, she just knew she wasn't going to like it.

"I'm sorry," the officer said, "but this used to be the Smith farm. My grandparents bought it from them back in the Sixties, and they renovated it."

Not the Morgans?

Disoriented, she grasped the railing to steady herself. An icy ball formed in the pit of her stomach as a feeling of dread crept over her. She licked her lips. "What do you mean, *back* in the Sixties?"

As if he were trying to assemble a puzzle without all the pieces, Jake stared down at her. "What do you mean, *what do I mean*?"

A hollow, empty space formed in her chest as she studied Jake's bewildered frown. Her tight grip on the hope that this was all a dream slipped. If she was dreaming, she wouldn't catch the woodsy scent of Jake's cologne, would she? If she were fast asleep in her bed, the crisp, spicy perfume of pine wouldn't tickle her nose. She'd never had a sense of touch in her dreams, but the velvet trim on her coat felt soft against the back of her neck, the wooden door firm beneath her touch. Drawing in a breath, she searched Jake's face for answers.

She could hardly get the words out, but she forced herself to ask, "What year is it… now?"

Jake's head canted. "It's 2016."

"Not 1945?" Her breath escaped in a whoosh. How was it possible that she'd traveled a lifetime into the future? There had to be some reasonable explanation. She glanced up, hoping Jake would offer one, but the deputy only continued to stare at her while concern and disbelief swirled across his face. She steadied herself. "The way you're looking at me… you don't believe me, do you?"

"I, um…" In a gesture that meant the same now as it had seven decades ago, Jake shrugged. Rather than answering her directly, he stepped around her to open the door. "Why don't we go inside?"

And with little other choice, she did.

As soon as she stepped across the threshold, though, she knew she'd made a mistake. Her grandmother used to say that eavesdroppers never heard anything good about themselves. That old adage proved true again, and Hanna's cheeks warmed as voices drifted down the hallway from another room. She glanced at Jake while one woman worried aloud about his decision to bring someone he didn't know into their home. The deputy's shoulders bunched. His posture stiffened. He'd overheard the conversation, too. Wishing she didn't have to choose between invading someone else's home or going to jail, she lingered near the door. While she pretended that wiping her feet on the mat required her full concentration, Jake headed down the hall. At the doorway to the living room, he cleared his throat. The chatter he'd interrupted stopped immediately.

Jake cleared his throat again. "So, everybody. Say hi to Hanna."

Though her feet dragged, she stepped to Jake's side when he beckoned her.

"Mom, Dad, Louise, Gwennie, this is Hanna," Jake said as if this were a perfectly normal day. "Hanna, meet Gretchen and Mark, my parents. That's my sister, Louise, in the green. The little bundle of energy on the couch there, that's my niece, Gwen, though everyone who loves her calls her Gwennie."

Hanna gave herself an imaginary pat on the back for keeping her smile firmly in place while the family stared at her like she was some kind of new bug under a microscope. Or rather, an old bug. One who didn't fit in their world.

Chapter Four

*M*orning sun glistened off a layer of fresh powder. The snow snapped and popped like dry cereal beneath Jake's boots as he trudged along the path to the main house where he planned to check on Hanna and his folks before he reported in at the station. Freezing temperatures sent tendrils of crisp cold beneath his uniform jacket, and, eager for a cup of hot coffee, he walked faster. Outside the kitchen door, he stopped to eye the wood pile. The supply of firewood had gotten low. He made a note to spend some time alone with an ax before nightfall.

In the mudroom, he shrugged out of his jacket, hung his coat on the convenient rack, and stamped the snow from his boots on the mat. It didn't matter that he was over thirty, gainfully employed, and living on his own. His mom would still have his hide if he tracked snow and ice across her hardwood floors.

Warmth spread through his chest as he listened to

the familiar sounds of the family at breakfast. As usual, something troubled Louise—ever since her marriage had fallen apart, she had an urge to control everything about her life. His lips twisted into a rueful grin. Right now, his little sister wasn't the easiest person to live with, but their folks were just the medicine she needed. They'd have Louise back to her usual lighthearted self before too long.

Someone rustled the paper, and his grin deepened. In all likelihood, his dad sat in his usual spot closest to the fireplace where he pretended to read the paper. Meanwhile, his mom would be flitting about the roomy farmhouse kitchen, making sure everyone started the day with a hearty breakfast. Smiling, he rooted around in his pocket until he came up with a coin. He tucked it into his uniform sleeve before, rubbing his hands together, he rounded the corner and entered the room.

"Well, you could be a little more charitable." At the stove, his mother shoveled bacon onto a platter with an economy of motion while she addressed Louise over her shoulder.

Snagging a crisp slice from the pile, Jake gave his mom a peck on the cheek on his way around the wide counter to the spot where his niece sat.

"Mom, I'm not being uncharitable!" Louise slid a bowl of oatmeal in front of Gwennie. "It's just… you know. A little weird, you have to admit. Where'd she *come* from?" She broke the corner off a croissant. Nibbling on it, she continued. "We don't know. And now she's here? In our house?"

Gwennie dumped a spoonful of brown sugar on her oatmeal. "If she has amnesia, will she forget she met us last night?"

Jake traded eye rolls with his dad. The conversation was far too adult for little-girl ears. Which made this the perfect time for a distraction. "Good morning, squirt." He ruffled Gwennie's curls. "Want to see some Christmas magic?"

Just as he'd known she would, Gwennie responded to his offer with a searching look. In answer to her wordless questions, he showed her his empty palms. Then, executing the sleight of hand trick he'd been practicing, he reached behind her ear.

"Abracadabra!" He grinned as he withdrew his fingers. He held up a quarter. He made sure Gwen had a good look at it before he tapped it to the little girl's nose.

"How'd you do that, Uncle Jake?" Her eyes sparkling, his niece snagged the coin.

"Do what?" He feigned an innocent expression. "I'm not the one who needs to wash behind her ears."

While Gwennie thoughtfully tugged on her ear and sifted her fingers through her hair in case he'd hidden another coin in her curls, Jake grabbed a mug from the cupboard over the coffeepot. Helping himself to a cup of his mom's special brew, he inhaled. His nose filled with the spicy scent of cinnamon and home.

"Not so much sugar on your oatmeal, Gwennie," Louise admonished when her daughter reached for seconds.

"But will she, Mom?" Gwennie spun the coin on the table.

Jake's dad peeked at his only grandchild over the sports page. "She seemed okay to me. Except for the clothes."

Relieved of the immediate need to add his two cents' worth to the discussion, Jake leaned against the counter and drank.

But like a dog with a bone, Louise refused to let the topic drop. "Dad," she said, unmindful of the faint note of exasperation that had crept into her voice, "no one just *lands* in Central Falls without knowing how."

"Now, dear, she's perfectly nice." His mom, dressed and ready for the day despite the early hour, did her best to calm his sister's concerns. "I'm sure there's a perfectly good explanation for what happened."

"Besides," Gwennie protested, applying the insistent logic that only an eight-year-old could manage, "she didn't *land* here. She's *from* here."

"And that's another thing." Undaunted, Louise wrapped her fingers around a Christmas mug. "Has anyone ever seen her before? Or heard of her?"

Guessing that was his cue to join the conversation, Jake pushed away from the counter. "Hush. What if she walks in and hears all this?" he admonished. Though his gesture took in the whole room, he aimed the comment at his sister. "Let her rest, get her bearings, and we'll all get to know her soon enough."

Instead of looking properly chastised though, Louise gave him the same self-sure look she'd mastered when they were kids. "Aren't you supposed to have just a *little* professional skepticism?"

Ready with a quick retort, he clamped his lips closed over it when his mom spoke again.

"There's nothing wrong with having a trusting spirit."

And just like that, the conversation was over. Both he and Louise had learned to recognize that note of finality when their mother used it. As if to confirm it, his mom gave his shoulder a firm pat.

Then, like a general surveying her troops, his mom stood at one end of the kitchen counter and studied the breakfast she'd been preparing while they'd talked. Steam rose from a platter of scrambled eggs. Pats of fresh butter fanned out in circles on a plate beside a mound of fresh-from-the-oven sweet rolls and croissants. The meaty smell of bacon filled the air. She gave the array a quick nod of approval. "Why don't I go in and check on her? See if she's awake."

Already in motion, she paused long enough to pin her daughter with a look that had never failed to get results. "Now *you* all be polite. Remember, she's a guest in our house."

When Louise pressed her lips together, Jake knew the matter had been settled… for the time being. He took a last swig of coffee, and, with a glance at his watch, followed after his mom. He caught up with her in the hallway, where colorful poinsettias and greenery played well against the white staircase with its dark trim.

"Hey, Mom. I was wondering, were there ever Christmas lights on the old gazebo? On the square?" The question had been troubling him ever since he'd driven Hanna home.

"Christmas lights on the gazebo?" Gretchen ran a hand through curls she professed to hate, though he liked the way they softened the angles of her thin face. "No, I don't think so. Why do you ask?"

"It's nothing. Just something Hanna said on the drive out here yesterday. She was talking about how she used to go caroling and how pretty the gazebo would be if it were all decorated."

"Whew! You couldn't put just any old lights around that building. They'd have to be extra large or you wouldn't be able to see them. It'd cost a pretty penny to do it up right."

"Yeah, well. It was just a thought." Jake skimmed one hand over his uniform shirt as he swallowed his disappointment. Why had he even asked? It wasn't like he believed Hanna's preposterous story that she'd mysteriously arrived here from 1945. Much as he wanted to help their guest, his sister had made a valid point—he needed to maintain his objectivity. He cleared his throat. "Don't worry about it. I have to get to the station."

"You're not staying for breakfast?"

"Can't this morning. But I'll be back in time for dinner." He leaned down so his mom could buss his cheek. "Tell Dad he can take it easy today. I'll replenish the wood pile when I get in this evening."

With a nod, Gretchen continued on toward the guest room while Jake headed for the coat rack.

"Hanna? You awake, dear?" At the end of the hall, his mom rapped on the door. It opened with a soft squeak. Cautious footsteps sounded as he pulled his bulky coat from its hook.

"Jake!"

It wasn't often that concern tainted his mom's voice. When it did, she usually had good reason. Jake replaced his jacket on the hook and sighed.

Had bringing Hanna home with him been a mistake after all?

Hanna threaded her fingers through her hair and gave her curls a sharp tug. Pain—sharp and intense and *reassuring*—seared her scalp. She relaxed her grip and hurried down the sidewalk. At least *she* was real. After stumbling out of the building that had once been her home, she hadn't been sure there for a minute.

But what *was* going on? When had her house been turned into a store? What had happened to the furniture she and Chet had so carefully chosen for each room? Where were the pots and pans, the dishes she'd used to fix their meals? Where was her photo album, the only thing she had left of the man she loved?

Panic bubbled in her chest. She fought it by clutching her arms tighter while she hurried down Main Street. Her whole world had been upended ever since she'd taken shelter in the shed. But she knew how to fix things. She had to get to the hospital. She had to. If she could only see the Franklin Memorial Hospital sign, touch the building's red bricks, duck into the locker room and run her fingers over her locker—if she could do those things, then she wouldn't feel like she'd lost her mind anymore.

On the street, the horn on one of those newfangled cars honked. Something chirped, and, right in front of her, a car's trunk opened all on its own. Footsteps sounded on the sidewalk behind her. She glanced over her shoulder. The woman who'd been following her ever since she'd run out of Organic Planet ducked into an alcove.

Hanna picked up her pace. In her haste, she stepped from the curb straight into a puddle of melted snow. "Oh, darn." She sighed as an icy wetness soaked her hose. She stomped her feet. Oh well, she wouldn't melt. And there were a whole lot worse things than getting her stockings wet. Finding yourself in a dream and not being able to wake up, no matter what you did—that was worse. The dark despair she felt every time she thought of Jake's face yesterday when he'd told her it was 2016—that was definitely worse. Walking into her own home and learning that every trace of her life had been erased, replaced by something called Organic Planet—that was bad enough to make her scream.

She hadn't, but she *had* cried. Honestly, who wouldn't under the circumstances?

Though the nursing supervisor would have a thing or two to say about her posture if she saw her, Hanna hunched forward. She kept her eyes aimed down, her focus on the sidewalk so she wouldn't have to see people staring at her as she passed. Only a little farther. The hospital was just around the corner and halfway down the next block. Once she reached it, once she spoke to Dottie and saw Frank and Julia, everything would be all right again.

Except… the hospital wasn't there.

Outside the place where the hospital ought to be, she stopped and stared. Oh, the red brick looked the same. She scanned the second floor. That window, right there, that was the window where Toby had waved goodbye to her, and she'd made a goofy face. And over there, those trees… If she squeezed her eyes tight and tilted her head just right, she could almost imagine the tall cedars as the tiny saplings they'd been the last time she'd seen them. But the sign over the wide double doors announced that the building she knew as the Franklin Memorial Hospital now housed the Cook Public Library. When had that happened? Defeat spread its strength-sapping fingers through her.

"Hanna."

She jerked at the sound of Jake's voice. Straightening, she pointed an accusatory finger at the building. "What happened to the hospital?" she demanded.

"There is no—"

"The hospital!" She didn't think she could stand it

if one more thing from her life disappeared. "This is supposed to be the hospital!"

"It's not, though, is it?"

As if to make Jake's point, a man carrying a stack of books emerged from the building.

"Oh, Jake, I don't know what's going on." She shoved a wayward curl out of her face. "Nothing is the way it's supposed to be. And people, like that woman there…" She pointed to the stranger in the brown wool coat who'd been following her all morning. "I don't know if she wants to steal from me or have me committed to an insane asylum."

"Her? That's just Belinda Jones." At Jake's friendly wave, the woman turned around and sped in the opposite direction. "She's always butting into everyone's business, but she's harmless."

When Jake turned to face her again, the look in his warm brown eyes hardened. "But you can't go wandering off or making a scene wherever you go. It worries people. My mom was frantic when you weren't in your room this morning. And calls have been coming into the station about a deranged woman running all over town. That has to stop."

Jake was right about one thing: she had been acting a bit odd. "I, I'm sorry if I caused you any trouble. I didn't mean to upset anyone. I'm just trying to go home."

"I know," Jake murmured. He placed a comforting arm around her shoulder. "I know this has all been upsetting, but we'll sort it all out eventually. How about we take a walk?"

A walk through the park sounded like a good idea. Having someone on her side, someone to confide in, even better. She couldn't keep her thoughts, her fears, bottled up for another second. If she did, why, she'd just explode.

"I should have told you I was leaving but I... I couldn't sleep. All night, all I could think of was, if I could just get home! Somehow *home* would make everything normal again. But now my home is a..." Shaking her head, she sank onto a park bench. Discovering that someone had stripped her house of everything she owned had nearly made her wacky. Worse, nothing in this new world made sense. "I don't even what 'gluten free' is."

On the seat beside her, Jake gave a rueful smile. "Most of us don't."

"And then I thought of Dottie. I thought, if could get to the hospital—" She searched Jake's face and saw that his eyebrows had knitted the way they did when he didn't understand. He'd been doing that a lot, ever since she'd met him.

"The hospital. You mentioned that before."

"Today's my friend Dottie's shift. She's one of the smartest people I know. I thought, if I could just talk to her, she'd explain everything that's happening, and somehow it would all make sense. But... Dottie is gone. Everything I've ever known is... gone." She spread her hands. "I don't know what's happened to me. None of this"—her gesture took in the weather-beaten gazebo, the trees that were too tall, the cars that looked so strange—"is real. Am I dreaming? Or have I lost my mind? Or… what?"

"It must be really scary for you." Compassion shone like a beacon in Jake's eyes.

"I've seen the way everyone looks at me. Like I'm crazy. Or worse—lying." No one believed her. Not the woman who'd been following her. Or the sales clerk at… what was the name of that store again? Organic Planet, that was it. She'd seen Sarah roll her eyes, had overheard Louise's doubts. And to tell the truth, if she'd been in their shoes, she would've felt the same way.

"You were right about our farm being the Morgan place."

Her head snapped up. "What?" she gasped.

"I checked the property records. It *was* a dairy. Back in the Forties."

"Do you believe me, then?" she asked, hesitant. She held her breath. She couldn't deal with this on her own. She needed help. But that meant someone, at least one person, needed to believe she was telling the truth. Was Jake that person?

"I, um, believe we're going to find out what happened."

When doubt flickered in Jake's eyes, she slumped forward. "I'm really scared," she admitted more to herself than anyone else.

"You're going to be okay." Reassurance and certainty filled Jake's voice. The hand he placed on top of hers chased away some of the chill that had crept into her heart. "I'm here to make sure of that. Okay?"

She inhaled a thready breath. She still didn't understand how she'd gotten here or if she could ever get home, but at least Jake had offered his help. That was all she could ask of him. Of anyone.

Jake pulled away the tarp that protected the wood pile from snow and sleet. This far into the winter, moisture had frozen the logs together. He wrestled an armload loose while, behind him, the door to the main house slammed shut. He didn't need to turn around to know whose footsteps sounded across the porch. Or to know that something—something *he'd* done—had gotten under Sarah's skin.

And not in a good way.

The fact that he'd brought Hanna home to his parents probably still bothered her. Though why she cared one way or another was a mystery he couldn't solve. He adjusted the load of wood in his arms and trudged through the snow to the old stump he and his father had used as their chopping block for as far back as he could remember.

"The chief's not happy," Sarah announced, taking her stance at his side.

Jake nodded. *Tell me something I don't know.* After piling the logs on the ground, he headed back for another load.

"We fielded calls from concerned citizens all over Central Falls when Hanna—if that's even her real name—was out wandering around this morning. People want assurances that she's not dangerous, but we don't know enough about her to say whether she is or she isn't."

"What is she, a hundred-and-ten soaking wet?" His arms once more full, he retraced his steps. He stole a quick glance at Sarah. Twin spots of color bloomed on her cheeks just like they did whenever he did or said something that troubled her. Adding his logs to the stack, he gave her his best, reassuring smile. "Trust me, she's not dangerous."

"You've gotta take her in, Jake," Sarah insisted. "You're going to get in trouble if she disappears for real next time."

Though learning that she worried about him ignited a warm glow in the pit of his stomach, he had to quash Sarah's fears about Hanna. "She wasn't trying to run away." He hefted a log and squared it away on the stump. "She was just trying to figure out what happened. Like we all are."

"Yeah?" Sarah cocked a hip. "So what's her angle?"

"There's no *angle*." He brought the ax down with a bit more force than necessary. Why couldn't she see that Hanna needed their help? "I believe her."

"Oh, she just dropped out of the sky? From 1945?"

Well, when she put it that way, it did sound kind of silly, didn't it?

He glanced over one shoulder in time to see the disbelief that clouded Sarah's eyes and hurried to correct himself. "I mean, I believe she believes it."

They needed to give Hanna the benefit of the doubt. The woman had enough problems just dealing with the disappearance of huge chunks of her life. Not that he believed for a moment that she'd gone to sleep one night and woken up nearly three-quarters of a century later. Rip Van Winkle *was* a just a fairy tale.

"Yeah, right." Sarah scuffed one boot through the snow. "Look, you'd better find something to support her story or some proof of who she really is, or you're going to start sounding as wacky as she does."

"Thanks for the vote of confidence." He grimaced. He wished Sarah would give Hanna a chance. His training partner came as close to perfect as a person could be, but her cynical nature sometimes kept her from seeing the good in people. Take the kid they'd spotted riding down Main Street with a video game strapped to the back of his bike the other day. Certain she'd nailed a thief, Sarah would have arrested the boy if Jake hadn't asked to see his receipt. Turned out, the kid had saved his allowance for a year to buy his younger brother a special gift for Christmas.

"That's what I'm here for."

Jake smothered a grin. Despite the flip response, he knew he'd made his point. "See you tomorrow," he called, planting the ax head in the snow and leaning on the handle.

"All right." Heading for her car, she tossed the words over her shoulder without a backwards glance.

He grabbed another log from the pile. Standing it upright on the stump, he hefted the wooden handle over his head. In one fluid motion, he brought the ax head plunging down. The blade sliced into the wood, which split straight down the middle. He gathered the pieces and added them to a growing stack of firewood for the stove, the task as familiar as getting out of bed in the morning or brushing his teeth before he turned in at night.

Nothing was simpler, more ordinary than chopping wood, but for Hanna, nothing was simple or ordinary anymore. Why couldn't Sarah see that? Despite her innate cynicism, Sarah didn't ordinarily jump to conclusions, but she'd pegged Hanna as a con artist right from the start and, so far, he'd been unable to change that opinion.

Was something else going on with his partner? Some dynamic that he didn't understand?

He shook his head. Whatever had caused the tension between the two women, Hanna was a mystery unlike anything Central Falls had ever seen before. He meant to solve that mystery—no matter what the reason behind it—and he had a pretty good idea where to start.

Well before his shift the next morning, Jake pulled to a stop in front of one of Central Falls's most beautiful homes. Exiting the patrol car, he took a moment to appreciate the architect's sense of style. Symmetry showed in every detail, from the twin chimneys that stood guard over the house, to the stately columns on either side of the grand entryway. The town's leading citizen had extended that balance to the manicured trees and bushes that flanked the sidewalk. Lights twinkled from the pair of miniature Christmas trees on pedestals near the door. Thick strands of braided garland created a welcoming smile on the decorative railing above the covered entry.

The scene inspired him to look his best, so, straightening his jacket and squaring his shoulders, Jake strode from his vehicle and up the sidewalk. At the front door, he lifted a heavy door knocker shaped like a dog's head and let it fall. Almost instantly, a young man answered.

Relieved that he wouldn't have to bother the owner of the house, Jake got straight to the point. "I understand Mr. Cook owns the small storage shed near the gazebo. If I could borrow the key to it, there's a small matter I'd like to look into."

With a warm gesture, the man Jake recognized as Tobias Cook's assistant welcomed him into the foyer. "I don't suppose that'd be a—"

"Julius, who's there?" Tobias Cook's voice rose from a room off to the left.

"It's Deputy Stanton, sir." A warm smile lightened the seriousness of Julius' features as he glanced in his boss's direction.

"Show him in."

A moment later, Jake thanked his lucky stars that he'd spruced up a bit when he walked into a room lined from floor to ceiling with books. At Tobias's appraising glance, he drew his posture even straighter.

Closing the leather-bound journal in which he'd been writing, the older man stood. "Welcome, Deputy Stanton. Did I hear correctly?" Tobias tilted his head. "You want to look in the storage shed? It hasn't been broken into, has it?"

"Jake, sir." He shook the man's extended hand. "There haven't been any problems that I know of. It's just something I wanted to check out, sir."

"It wouldn't have anything to do with that young woman who's been wandering around town, would it?" Questions filled Tobias's intelligent blue eyes. "I overheard Belinda Jones and her husband talking about her this morning at the diner. Seems she's stirred up quite the fuss."

Jake blinked. Sarah had been right. People *were* talking about Hanna. He hurried to put Tobias's—and the town's—fears at ease. "Yes, sir. I don't believe she means anyone any harm, though. She says her name is Hanna Morse. She's staying at the farmhouse with my family till she gets her bearings. Right now, she seems a little confused about…" Jake shrugged, "… about a lot of things—where's she's from, how she got here, what year it is."

Tobias tapped his chin thoughtfully. "Happens to the best of us."

Jake glanced at the book-lined walls. People said Tobias knew more about the history of Central Falls than anyone around. Maybe he could shed some light on their visitor. "She says she once owned a house over on Elm Street, that she worked as a nurse in a hospital here in town back in the Forties." He sighed. "But that's a little far-fetched, seeing as she's close to my age. And Jessica Lipscomb is the only doctor in town."

"A hospital, you say?" Tobias's eyebrows quirked. "She must mean the library. There aren't many people around here old enough to remember that during the war that building was a hospital."

"She has her facts right, then?" He'd lived here all his life, and he hadn't known that the library had ever been anything else. How had Hanna known about it? He pulled a small notebook from his back pocket and jotted down a reminder to check the town records.

"Sure she does. After the war, the hospital stood empty for so long that people wanted to tear it down. But I thought Central Falls needed a nice library more than we needed another store front."

"That was a good decision, Mr. Cook," Jake agreed, belatedly realizing that the library must have been named after the man who'd deeded the building to the town. "I spent many an hour in the computer room there when I was a kid."

"Yes. Well…" Tobias gave his chin a thoughtful tug. "Have you been able to verify any other parts of her story?"

"That's what I'm trying to do now, sir. Hanna—Mrs. Morse—said she passed out or was knocked unconscious and woke up in the storage shed by the gazebo. I thought I'd check it out, see if I can find any clues to her in history there. That's why I'm here, to ask if you'd mind if I poked around a bit."

"Go ahead, son." Tobias extracted a key from the ring on his belt. His eyes twinkled merrily. "Just don't expect too much. Time travelers don't often leave clues to their past."

Time traveler? Surely, Tobias didn't mean to imply...

Jake tried the idea on for size. It sure would explain most, if not all, that Hanna had experienced... except for the fact that time travel didn't exist. He gave Tobias a probing look, but the older man only laughed politely, as if he'd told a joke that hadn't quite worked.

He saw himself out and, a short while later, he stepped into the tidy storage room at the edge of the town square. The usual assortment of rakes and shovels hung from hooks on the walls. A neat stack of empty sandbags stood in one corner.

At first glance, everything appeared as it should be, and disappointment stirred in his chest. He wasn't sure what he'd expected, but there was nothing out of the ordinary about the shed. Nothing except...

He reached for his flashlight and played it over the floor. Faint tracks in the dust indicated that a sturdy table had been moved across the room and positioned against the far wall. Above it, an open window louvered outward, providing enough space for someone to crawl through. A flash of color caught his eye, and he bent to retrieve a purse from the floor. He held the bag up to the light. Bright flowers in some kind of stitching decorated the cloth bag. Though he fought to remain aloof and professional, he couldn't deny the thrill of excitement that flowed through him. He'd seen pictures of purses like it on eBay. If he wasn't mistaken, they dated back to the early Forties.

Sure he'd found his first real clue to Hanna's identity, he tucked the bag under his arm. Hurrying, he latched the window closed, exited the shed, and locked the door. He'd have one of the other deputies drop the key back at Tobias's house. For now, he needed to get the purse back to the station, where he'd examine its contents for anything that would back up Hanna's story.

An hour later, he still poured over the items from the purse. For the tenth time in as many minutes, he removed the cap on a tube of lipstick and stared at a startling red that, according to Sarah, had gone out of fashion ages ago. He tapped a few keys on the computer screen and scanned through the manufacturer's history. The cosmetic company had folded in the Sixties. No help there. Picking up a vial of perfume, he rolled the thin blue bottle between his fingers. According to the internet, the cologne had been the most popular fragrance sold in the United States during World War II. He sniffed at the stopper. Hanna's scent filled his head, and he set the bottle aside just as the door to the squad room opened.

On the heels of a burst of cold air, Sarah entered the room. Struggling to maintain a professional demeanor, he tempered the smile that threatened whenever he saw her. She strode toward him.

"Nothing," she announced without preamble. "I spoke with my contacts over at the Department of Motor Vehicles, but it didn't get us anywhere." She slapped her clipboard on his desk as if eager to prove that she'd been right all along. "DMV records don't go back that far." Unclipping Hanna's license from her board, she fanned it against her fingers. "No photo. Convenient," she said with the barest hint of a smirk.

"Licenses didn't have photos in the Forties." He took the slip from her hand. The aged paper felt silky smooth to the touch. "In fact, until the Thirties, they didn't even have drivers' licenses."

Sarah perched on the corner of his desk. "Aren't you becoming the historian?"

"You can learn just about anything from the internet." With a click of the mouse, he brought up the site he'd been using for his research.

"Not everything." Sarah's smile turned smug. She pointed a neatly trimmed fingernail at Hanna's license. "She could have gotten this printed at any copy place. As for her getup—you can get those old clothes at the thrift store."

He lifted an eyebrow. "Why would she want to do that?"

"I dunno." Sarah flipped her ponytail over one shoulder. "Identity theft?"

That again? "Oh, come on." Sarah knew him better than that. If he'd had the slightest hint that Hanna was a thief or a con artist, he'd have never introduced her to his parents or let her anywhere near his niece.

"Louise said she was making herself *quite* at home. Maybe she's homeless, and she wants *you* to take her in."

"Sarah…" he began and stopped himself. What was it he saw glowing in her eyes? Was she… *jealous*? The idea knocked him back a bit. He thought he knew all of Sarah's moods, but this was something new, something different, something that had… possibilities. Hoping for a second glimpse, he studied the woman he'd known practically his entire life, but the emotion—if it had ever been there—had been replaced by Sarah's usual healthy dose of cynicism.

"Well, you tell me—what's your theory? She didn't just *drop in* from 1945." Sarah sifted through the items on his desk before she lifted the bottle of perfume. "Lune de Paris." She held the bottle beneath her nose and sniffed. Her lips pursed. "Paris Moon."

"Okay, stop playing with the evidence." He held out his hand and waited until she dropped the vial into his open palm.

"It's something to think about," she insisted as she slid from the corner of his desk and sauntered across the room to the coffee pot. "I'm just saying."

Jake held the thin bottle up to the light. Liquid sloshed against the glass sides, and he drummed the fingers of his free hand against the desk. Up till now, they'd been looking at Hanna as someone who either belonged in the psych ward or was trying to con them in some way. But what if there was another option? Tobias Cook had to have been joking when he'd mentioned time travel, but what if he'd latched onto something? According to Jake's research, Hanna's perfume had only been distributed in the United States for a few years. If he could prove this sample came from that time period, it would go a long way toward supporting her story. And if it wasn't, well, either answer would help him solve the riddle of Hanna Morse's true identity.

Pretty sure the lab could tell him all he needed to know, he carefully slipped the container into an evidence bag.

When Gwennie bit the tip of her tongue while she concentrated on threading the next berry onto her string, Hanna smiled. After all the distress she'd caused the Stantons by going into town on her own, she'd been sure Gretchen and Mark would ask her to leave when she'd returned to their house this morning. But instead of scolding her, the elder Stantons had welcomed her with open arms, insisted she eat breakfast, and given her a change of clothes.

Strange clothes, to be sure. Why, she'd never worn pants in her life, except to garden or ride her bicycle. Yet, these women wore them all the time. Even Jake's mom, Gretchen, wore blue jeans, and she had to be in her sixties. Hanna smoothed one hand down the seam of a pair of clingy leggings that hugged her legs tighter than anything she'd ever worn before. She wasn't sure she'd ever get used to the snug feel of the fabric against her skin, though she had to admit, that layering trick Louise had showed her worked wonders at keeping her warm.

How could anyone stay blue when they were surrounded by so much kindness?

And so, when Gwennie had peppered her with questions about her past, Hanna had chosen to share only her happiest memories. She'd had no idea that the little girl would insist on recreating all of her most treasured Christmas traditions. Or that they'd spend hours cutting out long strips of paper and gluing them together to make paper chains for the Stantons' Christmas tree. Gwennie's enthusiasm had quickly spread to Gretchen and Louise, too.

Now, hours later, they had all gathered in the kitchen. While Gwennie concentrated on sliding the next cranberry onto the nearly full string, Hanna took a moment to whisper a prayer of thanks for her good fortune. Her own house, with its wooden counters and tiny refrigerator, had never been as grand as this one, but the gingerbread houses she'd built weren't very different from the one that sat at the end of the Stantons' granite counter. Her stove had only had two burners instead of six, but the spicy mix of cinnamon, cloves and nutmeg that wafted from the simmering pot of mulled cider made the house smell like Christmas, just as it had in her much more modest home. She'd never even seen an electric beater before, but she had to admit, the invention took all the drudgery out of making cookies. And when Gretchen and Louise rolled out the dough and cut it into shapes, they used cookie cutters that looked much the same as the ones she'd used.

"Hanna, I need another cranberry, please."

"Oh!" Startled, she glanced down at Gwennie's open palm. Sorting through the berries left in the pan, she selected the plumpest, reddest one and handed it across.

"There!" Gwennie threaded it onto the string. "All done. What's next, Mom?"

"Maybe you could read or play with your toys." Louise slid a pan of cookies into the massive oven.

"All night? Mom, that's boring." Gwennie folded her arms across her small body.

Hanna frowned. This close to Christmas, it didn't seem right that they were all cooped up inside. "When I was a little girl, just about your age," she began, "I used to go caroling around the gazebo with my friends. Everyone came out for it. Seems like all the neighbors were there. We'd carol. We'd drink hot cocoa and laugh."

"That sounds like fun!" The tiny divot between Gwennie's eyebrows deepened as she concentrated on tying a big knot at the end of her garland. She turned to her mom. "Can I carol?"

"Kids don't go caroling anymore?" Hanna asked. It just didn't make sense that people had stopped doing something that brought so much joy to so many. Did they call it something different now than they had back then? So many other things had changed, she wouldn't be at all surprised if that had, too.

"I guess we just don't..." Louise looked up from the cookie she'd been frosting. In a motion so much like her brother's, she shrugged. "I don't know. I guess we've just never done it."

"Can we, Mommy? Can we go caroling?" Gwennie begged.

Louise traded looks with Gretchen before she answered, "Yes! We'll go soon. In fact, I have an idea of how to make it even better." She glanced around the kitchen like someone who'd just discovered a critical item that needed to go on the top of their to-do list. "But we'll need to decorate the gingerbread house tonight. Do you think you and Hanna could start on it while Mom and I finish up with these cookies?"

Gwennie's eyes sparkled. "Let's do it." She reached for Hanna's hand. "If that's okay with you, Hanna. It is, isn't it?"

"Of course it is. I'll get started making the icing right now." She smiled and stretched her fingers. Though she'd never admit it, she'd been itching for a chance to try out that newfangled electric beater.

An hour later, she frowned at the tiny splatters of frosting that dotted her apron. Handling the mixer required a skill she hadn't mastered, but given enough time and patience, she would. For now, though, she'd focus on passing down the traditions of the season to another generation. Hanna hovered over the little girl's shoulder, watching as Gwennie piped frosting onto the roof of the gingerbread house.

"There you go," she said, offering encouragement. "Like that. Careful."

Gwennie glanced away from the perfect half-moon she'd drawn. "And this makes it stick?"

"Sure does."

Doubt clouded the girl's pretty blue eyes. "Are you sure? What if it falls?"

"It won't." A good royal icing stuck like glue and dried rock hard.

"But how do you know?"

Memories of the gingerbread houses she'd made through the years flooded back. "Dottie and I used to make one every Christmas. But when the war started, we stopped because sugar was rationed."

"What is *rationed*?" Gwennie's tiny face scrunched while, at the stove, Gretchen frowned and Louise stiffened.

Darn it, Hanna breathed. What had she been thinking, talking about the war like that? No one needed to hear about men getting killed or the sacrifices the people they'd left behind had made. Hadn't Chet and others like him given their lives so children like Gwennie could enjoy their freedom without ever experiencing hardships like rationing? She shook her head. She needed to be more careful about what she said whenever she was around the girl.

I'm sorry, she mouthed to Louise. But she wasn't a bit surprised when the young mother announced that it was time for her daughter to go to bed.

"But, Mom," Gwennie whined. "It's early yet."

Hanna felt a smile tug on her lips. No matter how much time had passed, no matter how many new inventions had been created or how many traditions had fallen by the wayside, some things never changed. It warmed her heart to know that arguing about bedtime was one of them.

"Can Hanna read to me?" the girl pleaded when it finally sank in that her mother wasn't going to back down.

Louise gave a bowl of frosting another stir before she answered. "I guess you're going to have to ask Hanna."

"Of course. I would love to!" Reading bedtime stories was the least she could do to thank her new friends after all they'd done to welcome her into their home, their lives.

Once her granddaughter raced up the stairs to change into her pajamas, Gretchen looked up from the pan of gingerbread men she'd been icing. "Are you sure? You don't have to."

"Oh no," Hanna rushed to reassure her. "I want to. I was just…" An odd thickening in her throat stopped her from continuing. She took a deep breath. If Chet had come home from the war, would they be looking forward to sharing a Christmas like this one with their own child? She swallowed and tried again. "I've always wondered what Christmas would be like with a big family."

"A bit chaotic." Louise softened the dry comment with a smile.

"No. It's… perfect." Those pesky tears were back, and this time they'd brought friends. Hanna blinked them away. Determined not to dampen the holiday mood for everyone else, she brushed her hands on her skirt and escaped to the other room, where she spent the next few minutes reassembling her composure. By the time Gwennie charged back down the stairs and climbed up beside her in the comfortable chair closest to the fire, she had her emotions under control again.

"'It's a miracle,' the wise old woman told Lily," Hanna read aloud some time later. "But Lily frowned because she didn't believe in miracles. Outside, the snow fell silently and the only noise was the stomping of small hooves. The reindeer were impatient." She glanced at the drowsing child snuggled beside her and closed the book. "It's probably time for bed," she announced softly.

Gwennie traced one finger over the cover of the book. "Hanna, do you believe in miracles?"

Hanna shook her head. Not so long ago, another small child had asked her the same question. She'd thought she'd known the answer then, but things had changed, hadn't they? Was a miracle to blame for her being here, now? "Well, I don't know," she admitted. "I mean, I don't know what I think anymore."

"I do." The girl stared at her with the self-confidence that belonged only to the very young or the very old. "Mr. Cook says you should believe in everything with an open mind."

An open mind, huh?

She'd been struggling to do just that ever since she'd woken up in the shed, but she was no closer to figuring out why she was here or how she'd ever get home than she'd been then. "Your Mr. Cook must be a very smart man." He also sounded like someone she should talk to. Maybe he'd have some answers for her.

"He runs the science fair. He also turned an old building into the library." Gwennie shifted in the chair until she kneeled close to Hanna's ear. Cupping her fingers around her mouth, she whispered, "He paid for it himself. He's *exceedingly* wealthy."

Suddenly, something made sense. "That old building was my hospital. And it was just built before the war."

"Mr. Cook also believes in time travel," Gwennie confided as if sharing a huge secret. "He says just because we don't understand something doesn't mean it doesn't happen."

"He does?" She leaned forward, questions about the mysterious Mr. Cook on the tip of her tongue. But before she could question the child, her mother appeared in the doorway.

"Gwennie, time for bed," Louise announced in a tone that brooked no argument.

Hanna sank against the cushions while the little girl scrambled from the chair. This Mr. Cook sounded more and more like someone she wanted to meet.

And the sooner, the better.

Chapter Five

"Thanks, Dr. Lipscomb. I appreciate the advice." Jake hung up the phone. Thoughtfully, he crossed to the rack next to his stereo. He ran a hand over the covers of the CDs until he found the one he wanted. After pulling it out, he checked the recording dates and smiled. This would do.

Four days ago, he and Sarah had responded to the call to help a woman in distress in downtown Central Falls. They'd been working to solve the mystery of Hanna Morse ever since. Yet, none of their leads had panned out. Last night, he'd stayed up reading missing person reports until his eyes crossed. The effort had been in vain—no one fitting Hanna's description had been reported missing anywhere in the state. This morning, he'd scoured the national databases for information and drawn another blank. It was as if Hanna had never existed. In desperation, he'd turned to the internet and, while he hadn't found anything that shed light on her identity, he had stumbled across something that might help her regain her memory. Now, with Dr. Lipscomb's approval, he'd see if it worked.

Well, there was no time like the present. He shrugged his coat on and headed up the hill to the main house.

Wiping snow from his boots in the mudroom, he listened to the sounds of silence. Where was everyone? He wandered from the back hall through the kitchen to the living room.

There, Hanna stood in front of the Christmas tree, a vacant expression on her face. She looked so lost and forlorn that a fresh desire to help her washed over him. Hating to interrupt her reverie, but anxious to find a solution to her predicament, he walked into the room.

"Hey!" he said, pitching his voice low so he didn't startle her. "I didn't think anyone was home."

"Just me," she said with a sigh. "Your mom and Louise took Gwennie into town. They said they had an errand to run before we went caroling tonight." Her smile wobbled a little as she turned to face him.

"Are you okay?" He stepped closer.

"It's all a little strange." She paused as if she had a secret to share but wasn't sure she should. "A lot strange," she admitted at last. "Sometimes, I look around at all this"—her expansive gesture took in everything from the handmade broom by the fireplace to the red bow centered on the curtains—"and the tree, and your great family, and I feel… happy."

"Well, there's nothing wrong with that." Wasn't that what everyone wanted—to find happiness?

"But then, I feel guilty for being happy." Hanna held out her empty palms. She heaved a sigh. "Oh, I'm not explaining this well."

In his most reassuring tone, he said, "It's okay."

"It's just, well, I've never known a Christmas like this. All the beautiful decorations. So many presents under the tree. It wasn't like this back when, um, where, where I was before." Her face mirrored her confusion. She shook her head and tried again. "The war, it changed everything. But even before that, I never had a big family." She brightened. "I had my husband, Chet. We were friends since childhood. We always knew we would be married, and, finally, we were—right before the war. And then, then he was gone. And now..." Her smile collapsed. "*Everything is gone.*"

Unable to stand her defeated look, he offered what little comfort he had to give. "Not everything. You have all of us. And this Christmas." Whether or not they ever learned who she really was, at least he could give her that much.

The remark earned him a halfhearted smile that reminded him why he'd come looking for her in the first place. He tapped the CD against the palm of his hand. "I had an idea. Are you willing to try it?"

Hanna tilted her head, considering. "I guess I am."

Okay, her willingness wasn't a hundred percent, but sometimes, you had to work with what you had.

He snapped the case open. "Here," he said, holding the CD up for her to see. "This is one of my favorites."

"What is it?" Questions bloomed in Hanna's eyes as she stared at the silver disk.

"What, this?" he asked, unable to hide his confusion. He'd expected her to ask about the performers, but unless he was mistaken, she had no idea what he held in his hand. "It's a, um—" How could he put it so she'd understand? "They used to be called *albums*." He studied her face closely. Relief washed through him when understanding dawned in her blue eyes. Crossing to the unit on the table by the window, he inserted the disk and hit the Play button. In seconds, the familiar strains of "I'll Be Home For Christmas" rose from the speakers.

"Oh!" Hanna's mouth formed a small oval. "That's the new tune Bing Crosby sang for the troops." She stared at the stereo unit. "And it's still popular after all this time?"

"Yep. Sure is. Most well-known singers have recorded it. But I chose the instrumental version just for you." That part had been Dr. Lipscomb's suggestion. She'd said Hanna would be more apt to respond to the melody than a modern-day singer. Watching Hanna tap her toe in time with the music, he guessed Dr. Lipscomb had been right. "Can you dance?"

"It's been a while," Hanna murmured though she slipped into his arms as if her last spin around the dance floor had taken place only yesterday.

Ballroom dancing wasn't really his thing. He

concentrated on avoiding Hanna's toes while he hoped Dr. Lipscomb was right about the rest of what he'd found on the internet. The doctor had agreed that familiar tunes often triggered a new awareness in Alzheimer patients and others who'd suffered memory loss. Hanna's situation was a little different, almost as if she'd gotten lost in a story that kept going after she'd closed the book. Even more perplexing, she recalled that long-ago setting in precise detail. Something had to loosen her grip on the Forties. If a song might help, it was worth a try, wasn't it?

"It brings back memories," Hanna murmured.

Could music possibly be the key to unlocking her identity?

"Chet wrote the lyrics in a letter he mailed to me from the front," she mused. "Everybody loves this song."

Encouraged, he crossed his fingers and danced them across the room as the chorus played. But then, just when he'd started to think they were onto something, Hanna's footsteps faltered. The mist of memories faded from her blue eyes.

"It's all so strange," she said, looking up at him. "I don't think I'm going to be able to get used to this."

"I'll help you," he insisted. He wasn't about to let the opportunity to help Hanna slip away from him. "You can trust me."

Unfortunately, she didn't seem to be listening. He frowned when she stepped from his arms. A faint pink tinge stained her cheeks as she stared over his shoulder. What had caught her attention? Curious, he turned. He supposed he'd been so caught up in the experiment to help Hanna regain her memory that he hadn't heard the front door open or the shuffle of feet in the hallway. Warmth spread through his chest the moment he spotted Sarah standing there. His mom and sister came in right behind her.

"Hey, guys!" he started. But in his excitement to share the progress he and Hanna had made, he must have missed something because Sarah gave an exasperated, "Huh!" and stormed out of the room. Meanwhile, his mom and Louise crossed their arms and glared at him the same way they used to do when he was a kid and left the seat up.

The next thing he knew, both Louise and his mom had disappeared. Claiming a headache, Hanna didn't waste a single second but retreated to her room, as well. Jake blinked. He shifted his gaze to the empty doorway and fought the urge to scratch his head.

Since apparently no one wanted to talk, he exited the house with as much grace as he could muster. He'd been working on a railing for his back porch. A hammer, nails, and an afternoon of honest labor finished off the project, but brought him no closer to understanding why Sarah and the rest had gotten their feathers so ruffled. By then, though, he figured the dust had settled enough to visit the main house again.

This time, after trudging up the hill, he was fortunate enough to catch his mom alone in the dining room. From the amount of Christmas paper, ribbons, and tape that littered the table, she'd held a marathon wrapping session this afternoon. Wishing he'd known the agenda in time to help out, he snagged a piece of fruitcake from a plate on the sideboard. Although he never got the corners exactly right, he found every aspect of the gift exchange uplifting. Especially this year, with Gwennie there to share the magic and wonder of the holiday. He'd spent hours thinking of the best presents for everyone on his list. Imagining their faces when they opened their gifts always made the season a little brighter.

Speaking of which, he hadn't bought Sarah's present yet, and time was getting short. Leaning against the doorframe, he considered what to get her while he chewed on a piece of candied pineapple. Through the years, he'd given Sarah a lifetime supply of scarves and gloves, but what else did you give the woman who saw you as nothing more than her best friend's older brother?

He eyed his mom. Maybe she'd have a suggestion or two. He popped the last bite of cake in his mouth and decided to ask her, just as she looked up and spied him in the doorway.

"Jake!" His mom deftly covered a box in gift wrap and taped one corner. "I've been waiting to speak to you all afternoon. What was going on between you and Hanna earlier?"

"Nothing, Mom. It was innocent." He brushed a few crumbs from his fingers. "Dr. Lipscomb said music was a good way to jog a person's memory. I was just trying to make Hanna feel okay."

"Huh. I guess that could work." His mother turned the box sideways. "But if that's all it was, then don't tell me. Tell Sarah." She motioned him to hold the ribbon in place while she tied the bow.

Glad to help out, even if he only lent a finger, he closed the gap between them. "Tell Sarah what?" he asked, while his mom fussed with the bow until it was perfect. As far as he was concerned, there wasn't anything to tell. Sarah already knew he was doing his best to solve the mystery of Hanna's presence in Central Falls.

His mom's lips straightened into a thin line. "Oh, Jakey, you can see how she looks at you," she said, as if he ought to know exactly what she meant.

"Sarah? Oh, Ma. Don't be silly," he protested while his heart skipped a beat.

Does Sarah have feelings for me?

No, he shook his head. His mom had to be wrong. Outside of their professional relationship, Sarah rarely gave him so much as a moment of her time. When she did, it was usually just to tease him without mercy. Yet, he wondered what had prompted his mom to make the comment. He had started to ask when Louise burst into the room.

She barreled toward him. Thrusting an odd-looking sweater into his hands, she spun. "What do you think?" she asked, giving them both a chance to view the old-fashioned coat and hat she wore.

"Ooooh!" His mom's face broke into a wreath of smiles. "That's going to be perfect!"

Jake let his gaze swing between the two women. Was that honest-to-goodness happiness on his sister's face? That didn't happen often these days. In fact, he was pretty sure he hadn't seen her express genuine interest in anything outside of her daughter since the day Louise had arrived on their doorstep with everything she owned loaded in the back of her minivan. So far, she'd refused to talk about the breakup, and he'd respected her need for privacy. Once the holidays were behind them though, he'd sit his sister down for a long, overdue chat. Then he'd go find that ex of hers and teach him a lesson about the proper way to treat his sister.

But that was for another day, another time. Today, he'd just enjoy the moment.

"Hmmmm," he said, willing to go along with anything that made his mom and sister happy. "Okay, what are you two girls up to?"

"It was Louise's idea," his mom insisted.

"It was Hanna's inspiration. We're all going to go out caroling tomorrow. Like an old-fashioned Christmas." Beaming, Louise giggled.

"In this?" Giving the sweater his most dubious look, he held it up to the light.

"Yes, in that." Louise poked his middle. "Jake, you wouldn't believe it. We ducked into the pawn shop today to ask if Hanna had visited the store to buy any clothes—"

"'Fess up—you were suspicious," his mom put in. "I told you that wasn't nice."

"I was just being careful." A defensive frown flickered across Louise's face.

Refusing to let anything dash cold water on his sister's good mood, Jake nodded agreeably. "Believe me, I'm running a thorough background check on her. I'll let you know if I find the slightest thing out of the ordinary."

Unless you consider it out of the ordinary to have no history whatsoever.

"Thanks, Jake. As I was saying…" The tiniest hint of a frown slipped from Louise's face. A look of wonder and excitement took its place. "The man at the pawn shop hadn't seen Hanna. But he had this marvelous picture of the gazebo, all decked out with lights and a Christmas tree. There was even a star on top. It was beautiful. Just the way Hanna described it. And it got me to thinking. Wouldn't it be wonderful to recreate some of the Christmas traditions she remembers? So, that's what we've done. She and Gwennie made paper chains and garlands from cranberries and popcorn for the tree yesterday. Then, before lunch, Hanna showed Gwennie how to make the most marvelous gingerbread house—wait till you see it. And tomorrow, we'll all go caroling together down on the square. It'll be fun."

"I just wish we knew where those old decorations for the gazebo had gotten off to. It'd be nice to see it all lit up again, like in the picture," Gretchen said wistfully.

Jake shook his head. "It's been seventy years, Ma. I'm sure they're long gone by now."

"Well, we don't have the lights, but we can carol," Louise said firmly. She looked him up and down. "So, you're in?"

"I don't know," he answered with a teasing grin that usually got a rise out of Louise. Sure enough, his sister tossed a piece of popcorn at him. Batting it down, he held the brown sweater to his chest. It looked like a good enough fit. Even if it hadn't been, he'd wear it to go caroling with his family.

"You said you wanted to make Hanna feel comfortable, didn't you? You should come with us," his mom said, as if the matter hadn't already been decided. She lifted one eyebrow along with the packages she'd wrapped. On her way out the door, she tossed another bit of sage advice. "And invite Sarah. Tell her that you're sorry."

"Sorry for what?" He grabbed a handful of popcorn. Sorry for trying to help someone who obviously needs help?

"Are you a dope?" Louise placed both hands on her hips and pinned him with the same look she used on Gwen whenever his niece refused to do as she was told.

"What?" Oh, he knew perfectly well what Louise meant. Only, his sister didn't know Sarah as well as she thought she did. The two women might drown their sorrows in a cup of hot chocolate together, but Louise didn't share the same squad car with her friend. She didn't work with Sarah day in and day out like he did.

If Sarah had fallen for him, he'd be the first to know about it. He was sure of it.

"You saw her face." Louise stamped one foot.

"Okay, what is this?" Figuring the sly glint in his sister's eyes meant in about two seconds he'd be wearing all the popcorn in the bowl, he took a backward step. "Is this like some secret female language I'm missing?"

Just as he'd known it would, the remark got under Louise's skin. Seconds later, he found out his sister's arm was a lot stronger than he'd thought it was when a kernel of popcorn bounced off his forehead. Before he could return the favor, Louise flounced out of the room, mumbling something about men and idiots.

Chapter Six

At lunch the next day, Jake stared across the squad room at Sarah. Was it even remotely possible the perky blonde had feelings for him? Or were his mom and his sister reading whatever they wanted to see into the situation?

Not that it mattered. Even the possibility that Sarah was interested had stirred up thoughts he'd never considered before. The kind that had robbed him of his sleep.

He'd spent the night walking the floor, examining the possibility of pursuing a relationship with Sarah from every angle. He'd thoroughly scrutinized every single minute he'd spent with her—from the moment she'd joined the force to yesterday, when she'd stormed out of his parents' living room. Through it all, he hadn't found so much as one sign that she viewed him as anything more than her best friend's annoying older brother. Having Hanna around hadn't helped matters—not one iota. If anything, Sarah had grown even more distant and pricklier than ever over the last few days.

On the other hand, if both his mother and sister said Sarah's feelings for him were more than platonic, shouldn't he at least explore the possibility?

He took a bite of the hamburger that could have been made of ground sawdust, for all he cared. Not even the crunchy French fries from the Central Falls diner tempted him, and they were world class. He might as well face it. Until he figured out where he stood with Sarah, he wasn't going to have much of an appetite.

But where should he start?

The situation called for a certain amount of finesse. He couldn't simply tromp over to her desk, demand to know if she'd fallen for him. What if she denied having any feelings for him at all? He'd look like some kind of fool if that happened. No, he'd better start with a safe subject. Then, after he saw how things went, maybe he could ask her out on a date. Or... or something. Gathering his courage, he munched on another tasteless French fry while he searched for a topic that wouldn't raise any alarms.

"I love snow," he blurted at last. "Do you like snow?" *The weather? Yeah, that was original.* He swallowed a groan. But now that he'd started, he couldn't stop. He had to keep on going. "White Christmas, and all that. That'd be nice. What about you? Hmm? Do you want snow?"

When Sarah continued staring out the window as if she hadn't heard a word he'd said, he abandoned his lunch and crossed the room to look over her shoulder. Had armed robbers descended on the store across the street? No. Everything was exactly as it should be beyond the big plate glass that overlooked Main Street. Last-minute shoppers hurried in and out of stores that had been decked out for the holidays. Looking as if she'd been sucking on a sour pickle, Mrs. Jones studied the window display at the Past & Present consignment shop. A couple of teenagers sped by, the wheels of their skateboards rumbling along sidewalks that had been shoveled and salted. The usual numbers of cars and trucks traveled through the heart of Central Falls.

His brow furrowed. Nothing out of the ordinary had captured her attention, so why was Sarah pointedly ignoring his questions?

Before he could ask her, she finally turned toward him. Her face pinched the way it did whenever she was deep in thought. "People are talking," she declared, her voice thick with innuendo.

About us? Nah, that wasn't it. "What?" He couldn't pretend he knew what she was talking about.

She pinned him beneath a dubious glare. "You know what."

"If I knew what, I wouldn't have asked what." Fighting an urge to squirm, he waited a beat. When she didn't respond, he shrugged. He guessed he'd have to spell it out for her. "So, *what?*"

"Her."

Oh. Hanna. He expelled the breath he hadn't realized he'd been holding. In case he needed another clue, Sarah's expression shifted into something that was halfway between a sneer and a frown.

"Sighing isn't denying." She shook a finger in his direction.

"What am I supposedly denying?" He'd be the first to admit that Hanna's sudden appearance in Central Falls had raised all kinds of questions. He was simply doing his best to answer them and to help her in the process.

"People are worried about who this stranger is." Turning away from him, Sarah slid onto the chair behind her desk. "We're supposed to be 'investigating,'" she said as she formed air quotes around the word, "but in reality, *one* of us has the hots for her."

"I do not." While the denial rolled off his tongue as only the truth could, he couldn't help but stare at Sarah. She really was jealous. His mom and Louise had been right all along. No wonder his partner hadn't been able to cut Hanna any slack. Sarah couldn't give Hanna the benefit of the doubt as long as she stared at their visitor through green-tinted goggles. He folded his arms across his chest and leaned against a nearby file cabinet while he took a second to absorb the rest of what his partner wasn't saying.

Sarah wouldn't be jealous if she didn't care about me, would she?

"You think I'm just your little sister's goofy friend, but, uh, I wasn't born yesterday."

"Oh, Sarah, come *on*..." She was one of the smartest, most intuitive people he knew. He was proud to have her as his partner, but could they ever have something... more?

"Nope." She shook her head. "I saw it with my own eyes. What am I supposed to tell people who are worried? That slow dancing is some new 'interrogation' technique?"

"I wasn't dancing." Well, technically he had been, but he'd had a very good reason for it. A very logical, scientific reason. One he'd love to tell Sarah all about, some other time. Right now though, he wanted to explore the idea that she might have feelings for him a whole lot more than he wanted to talk about Hanna. Hoping to put his partner's concerns about their visitor to rest so they could move on to other, more important things, he conceded the point. "Okay, we were dancing. But I... I was just trying to make her feel comfortable. That's all it was."

"Obviously," Sarah said dryly. "You should get a promotion for 'making the suspect feel comfortable.'"

There she went with the air quotes again. Enough already. Sarah's stubborn unwillingness to let go of her jealousy made it twice as difficult for him to tell his side of things, or to talk about what he really wanted to discuss—them. "Okay. Stop doing that."

"What?" she asked, giving him a doe-eyed look that was anything but innocent.

"That." He traced the two fingers of each hand through the air.

Sarah tapped a pencil against her desk blotter. "So, is she guilty?"

"No." He muffled an irritated grumble. In all the time Hanna had been staying at his folks', not a single thing had gone missing from the house. No matter what her reasons, Sarah knew better than to think he'd ever expose his mother, sister, or niece to someone who might bring them harm.

"A fraud?" Sarah struck another possibility off her list with another tap on the blotter.

"No." He hadn't been able to turn up a single piece of evidence that pointed to Hanna being anything other than she claimed to be—a woman who'd lost her way and was trying to get home. Except, more and more, he leaned toward accepting that in Hanna's case, the question he really ought to be asking wasn't *where* she lived, but *when*.

"Unhinged?"

"No," he answered, fighting a laugh. Hanna seemed as sane as the rest of them. More so, considering he was the one who'd started to think of time travel as a real possibility.

"Then what?"

"I don't know." He had a theory, but that was all it was, a theory. One so preposterous he knew better than to share it with Sarah. In her current mood, she'd probably write out two 1701s—one for Hanna, and one for him.

"Maybe you should dance with her some more," Sarah suggested slyly.

Okay, that remark was uncalled for. He had to put a stop to this before things got out of hand. "You're such a brat. You know that?" he said, falling into the teasing routine that felt as comfortable and familiar as an old shoe.

Wait a minute.

He took a second to regroup. Maybe that was part of the problem. Whenever things got weird between Sarah and him, they always resorted to banter and pranks like they were still on the grade school playground. But they weren't kids anymore. They'd long since outgrown the stage where they settled every argument by calling each other names or throwing snowballs at one another. They were adults. Adults whose feelings for each other might go deeper than simple friendship.

He gulped. Beneath her cynical outer shell, Sarah really cared about people, but did she care for him… that way? Was that what he wanted?

Nah, he shook his head. Sarah was his sister's best friend, his partner. He couldn't fall in love with her.

Or could I?

There was only one way to find out. But to do that, he'd have to take a chance.

"So, are you going to come tonight?" he asked, willing her to understand the seriousness of the question. A world of possibilities rested on her answer.

"What, caroling?" Sarah tilted her head. Slowly, realization widened her pretty blue eyes.

"Mm-hmm." He edged a little closer to her.

Uncertainty flickered across her face. "Are we gathering more information on the suspect?"

"Come on. Let that drop, will you?" It was time they both acknowledged that there might be a little something going on between them. "Just come."

For a long second, time stood still while he waited for an answer that could change things between them, could lead to something... more. At last, a tiny smile tugged on her lips. In that moment, he knew, he just knew, it would only take a little nudge to banish the last of her uncertainty.

"My mom wants you to be there," he added, not at all afraid to pull out the big guns if that was what it took to get Sarah to agree to show up. "Do it for her."

She canted her head. "Gimme the rest of your fries, and I'll consider it."

"Oh. That's a tough one." He gave the lunch he'd left sitting on his desk a mournful glance. Crossing the room, he grabbed the packet of fries and returned to Sarah's desk, bearing his bribe. The girl drove a hard bargain.

Hanna burrowed deeper into the gray wool coat. She skirted around a slick patch on the sidewalk and straightened her hat. Around her, Jake's family sported scarves, hats, and even shoes that looked like they'd come straight from the pages of the fashion magazine she'd bought off the newsstand just last week, back when she was in her own time. Despite temperatures that had been plummeting ever since sunset, warmth spread through her chest. The Stantons had shown far more kindness to her than she'd thought possible, much less expected. Take yesterday, for instance. In the middle of all their Christmas preparations, Gretchen and Louise had taken time out of their busy holiday schedule to visit a consignment shop, returning with armloads of what they called "vintage" clothes just to make her feel at home this evening. It really was touching, how they'd gone out of their way to welcome her into their lives. She smiled and raised her voice as the group of carolers burst into a rousing chorus of "God Rest Ye Merry, Gentlemen."

This, she said to herself, this was what Christmas was all about. The sights. The sounds. The companionship of friends and family. If only Chet were here to enjoy it, the evening would be perfect. But she couldn't think of Chet now. Dwelling on him was certain to dampen the mood and ruin the excursion Jake and his family had planned.

Speaking of Jake, where was he? Now that she thought of it, she hadn't seen him in quite a while. She glanced over her shoulder. The tall deputy had fallen behind the rest of the group. Anxious to tell him how much she appreciated everything he and his family had done to make her feel at home during the holiday season, she ducked beneath the awning at the entrance to the Birchdale Art Gallery, where she waited for him to catch up. But while the carolers moved on to their next stop, the deputy only stood on the corner as if he expected to meet someone. Curious, Hanna pulled the collar of her coat up around her neck.

A smile that highlighted Jake's best features spread across his face when Sarah stepped out of the darkness into the pool of light cast by the streetlight. In a tender gesture, Jake removed a hand-knitted scarf from around his neck and draped it around Sarah's shoulders. The answering glow on the young woman's face told Hanna all she needed to know.

And here, I fancy myself as a matchmaker. Why didn't I see that coming?

Why, Sarah and Jake were made for each other. They were just like she and Chet had been—lifelong friends who'd taken a while to recognize that they belonged together. The discovery sent joyful little shivers down her arms. She crossed her fingers and touched them lightly to her lips, then blew the couple a kiss for good luck. Pretending she'd just stopped to adjust the buckle on her shoe, she hurried to join the rest of the carolers when Jake, one possessive arm draped over Sarah's shoulders, moved up the sidewalk.

Several more singers had joined them by the time Hanna caught up with the rest of the group. Strains of familiar tunes filled the air as they traveled from one house to another, stopping here to sing "O Holy Night" and "White Christmas," and lingering in front of another home for eight verses of "Frosty the Snowman," an unfamiliar song to Hanna, while their breaths plumed in the cold air.

Laughing, the group gave themselves a round of applause at the end of the song. Hanna's grin widened when the singers launched into a rousing rendition of "Jingle Bells" on their way to the next house. But once they reached it, motion farther down the street caught her attention. She squinted at a woman who walked two dogs across the road. Seeing the golden retrievers with their long, shiny coats stirred a memory of a not-so-long-ago night. Quietly, Hanna stepped away from the group of carolers so she could keep the woman and her dogs in sight. She followed them for half a block before the woman mounted the steps into a house that, like the gazebo, looked different from how she remembered it.

Hanna paused at the gate. In the crisp breeze, a sign for Ruffin Kennels swung back and forth on hooks imbedded in the porch roof. "Ruffin," she murmured. Her memories sharpened.

"Hey. What's going on? Why'd you leave like that?"

She turned to find Jake standing at her elbow, concern etched in the faint tightening of the tiny lines around his eyes. She pointed at the house. "I was here. The night of the storm. I brought the dog back. His name was Ruffin." She scrutinized the wide front steps, the roomy front porch, the decorative trim on the door. "It's different," she acknowledged. "There, there wasn't a fence. But it is the same house." She nodded at the long driveway that led to a garage behind the home. "I parked my car over there. That night, the snow was blowing so hard…"

Questions bloomed in Jake's eyes. "You brought a dog here?"

She nodded. "He was lost. He came to my house. I found his ID tag and tried to call the owners, but there were people on the party line. They wouldn't get off."

"A party line. Boy, I haven't heard that term in a while." Jake kicked at a clump of snow.

She frowned. "You don't have them anymore?"

Jake pulled a small, rectangular device from his pocket. "Everyone uses cell phones now."

So that's what those were. She'd wondered. She leaned close enough to take a good look at Jake's. No wires trailed from the box in his hand. How did it work? She put a damper on her curiosity. However people spoke to one another through the cell phones, it'd be nice to have one in case of an emergency. Even better if it meant an end to waiting her turn to place a call, or trying to convince other customers to end their conversation before they were ready. She tapped one finger to her lips as a new thought occurred to her.

Would things have turned out differently if I'd had my own private line the night Ruffin appeared on my doorstep?

Silently, she nodded. If she'd reached the Bunces by phone, she wouldn't have ventured out in the storm. Not that it would change things now.

"Ruffin's address was on his tag, so I drove him here. Sue and Hal, the owners—they were so kind. They invited me to stay because the storm was bad." She glanced at the windows that were outlined in red and white by Christmas lights. "If I had stayed, I, I would never have driven my car into the snowbank, and… and I'd still be back where I belong."

The sound of hurried footsteps broke through the silence that hovered between her and Jake far longer than their breaths hung in the cold air.

"Hey! C'mon, you two." Louise emerged from the shadows into the light that spilled from the kennel's porch. "We're going to the square!"

Hanna pulled her shoulders erect. If she had managed to put on a brave face after Chet died, she wasn't about to let personal concerns ruin the lives of those around her now. "We're coming!" she announced.

Though worry flickered in Jake's eyes, he fell in step beside her when she walked smartly toward the square. As soon as she reached the others and slipped into her spot between Gwen and Louise, she knew she'd made the right decision. This was a night for caroling and glad tidings, not for moping about a past she couldn't change. It was a time for enjoying the camaraderie of those around her, even if she hadn't known a single person on the square before five days ago. It was a time for celebrating the season, and when the group began singing "O Come, All Ye Faithful," she forced her thoughts away from her troubles and joined in as the group gathered around the old gazebo.

"This is so much fun," Gwen declared when the song came to an end.

"I know!" Louise chimed in. "We need to do this every year."

Hanna summoned a cheery smile as Gretchen sidled closer.

"You've made us all so happy tonight, dear," Gwennie's grandmother whispered.

"Me?" Surprised, Hanna shook her head. "I didn't do anything at all."

"You *inspired* us. All of us." Gretchen's wave took in everyone from a couple of teenagers who'd tagged along after their last stop, to Jake and Sarah, who huddled together at the edge of the crowd.

A smile played across her lips. Gretchen was right. No matter how odd and out of place she felt, it was good to be a part of something bigger than herself. Tonight, traditions that had somehow gotten lost had been rekindled. If she had played some small role in that, well, that was a good thing, wasn't it?

Louise pointed toward the center of the small park. "It's such a shame they don't light the gazebo anymore."

Following her gaze, Hanna swallowed. Even in the dark, the structure had an ill-kept, shabby feel that broke her heart. "Oh," she gushed. "It was so beautiful! It would light up the whole square!"

"Well, we may not do that, but we've maintained other, important things," Louise offered. She turned solemn. "Here, I want to show you something."

When Louise took her hand, Hanna let herself be pulled forward. They'd only walked a few steps when Jake's sister stopped and pointed. "There. That's our war memorial. It honors all of the town's men who were lost in war."

"I know." Her parents had taught her the significance of the Central Falls war memorial. It had been the focal point of the town square for over a hundred years. The town's leading citizens maintained the marble plaque as a tribute to those who, like Chet, had made the ultimate sacrifice for their country, their loved ones. She moved closer. Slowly, she read the names of soldiers and sailors who'd died in battles near and far. At last, she came to a group of names she recognized—boys she'd gone to school with, friends who'd served alongside her husband.

Her throat tightened. Tears blurred her vision.

I should stop. I shouldn't look. Going on will only make me too sad.

But she owed them that much, didn't she? These men had given their lives for freedom. Reading each name, remembering each face, was the least she could do to honor their sacrifice, wasn't it? It was, and she braced herself as best she could. Slowly, her eyes drifted down. As if they had a mind of their own, her lips mouthed the names one by one.

And then she stopped.

Stepping forward, she brushed away the snow and ice while her heart pounded in her chest. When not so much as a dribble of ice remained, she ran down the list again.

And stared, frozen, at the space where Chet's name ought to be.

"Hanna?" Louise's voice drifted to her as if it came from far away. "Hanna, what is it?"

"Chet's name." She traced the list on the memorial with her fingers. "He died in the war, but... his name isn't here."

Vaguely aware of the slim arm around her waist, she let Louise lead her to a park bench. What did it mean? She repeated the question over and over while she sat, shivering from a cold far icier than the winter chill. Still pondering the possible answers, she barely paid attention when Jake and Sarah announced that they'd been summoned to Police Headquarters. On the ride home with the Stantons, she hunched into herself and stared out the window without seeing a thing. The moment they arrived at the farmhouse, she excused herself and went straight to her room while her head pounded with a single thought: Had Chet somehow survived after all?

At the edge of her bed, she stared at her wedding ring and felt her control shudder. Oh, what did it matter? She didn't have to put up a brave front, not when she was alone in her room.

Like every day since the day she'd received the telegram, waves of sadness rolled over her. Always before, she'd backed away from her grief. Tonight though, she felt too overwhelmed to fight, too tired to retreat. Her chest constricted until it hurt to breathe. Like floodwaters, tears rose in her eyes. This time, she made no effort to stem the tide. Her knees bent. She collapsed onto the bed. Her head in her hands, she let her tears flow.

Chapter Seven

"*I* just want to ask a few questions, that's all. Better safe than sorry, I always say."

Belinda Jones might mean well, Jake told himself, but her pinched face told him he and Sarah were in for more than just a few questions. An interrogation was more likely. He squared his shoulders and stood taller. At six-two, he towered over the town's biggest gossip, but he may as well have saved himself the effort. The tiny woman had compiled a long litany of problems with the way the Central Falls Police Department had handled their investigation into Hanna Morse. And, from the indignant expression on her face, Mrs. Jones wasn't about to leave until she'd voiced every single one of her many concerns.

"All I'm saying is that it's suspicious." She fisted both hands.

"Look—" Jake cupped his own hands in front of him. According to his instructor in the Hostage

Negotiation class he'd taken, the stance projected authority while it conveyed reassurance. If so, it didn't seem to have any effect on the irate citizen or her angry sputters. He firmed his tone and tried again. "Hold on, hold on."

But the woman's rant continued. Riding roughshod over his requests, she didn't even slow down long enough to draw a breath. Instead, she ticked items off on her fingers. "The crazy claims. The weird clothes. The brainwashing."

Oh, now you're just being ridiculous.

Although he'd been listening to Mrs. Jones's tirade for fifteen minutes, Jake smothered the protest that would guarantee him a reprimand if the chief ever got wind of it. "There's no brainwashing," he said in his softest, least threatening tone.

"Really?" Her two-handed gesture took in the fedora he'd picked up at Past & Present, as well as the Forties-style jacket his sister had given him.

Belatedly, he removed the hat from his head. "Look, I can explain if you'll—"

"Now, everyone is... *singing*!" Mrs. Jones put so much emphasis on the last word that she made singing sound like a worse crime than robbing a bank. "Ever since she got here, this entire town has been out of whack."

Even as he tried to once more calm the woman's fears, he could feel the edges of his patience start to fray. "Mrs. Jones, if you'll—"

"It's your job to get to the bottom of it." Her

voice ran on like a runaway freight train, one he was powerless to stop.

"But for some reason, she's staying at your house like she's some sort of guest." The little woman clasped her hands to her chest. "I am worried—"

A loud whistle rent the air. The sudden noise accomplished the one thing Jake had been unsuccessful in doing—it stopped Mrs. Jones in her tracks.

The epitome of restraint, despite the strident citizen in their midst, Sarah stepped from behind her desk. "Mrs. Jones," she said, one hand on the butt of her service revolver, the other perched on her hip. "I can assure you, the Central Falls Police Department has this situation *completely* under control. We take your concerns seriously." Sarah tilted her head in his direction. "Don't we?"

From her pointed look, he knew there'd be serious consequences if he failed to back her up. Well, he had no problem with that. It was, after all, what he'd been trying to say all along. "Absolutely," he agreed.

"And…" Sarah faced Mrs. Jones again, "we are looking into every angle of this." She waited a beat for her statement to sink in. "But now it's late," she continued. "When the department is ready to issue a statement, you'll be the first to know."

"Why don't you go on home now, Mrs. Jones," Jake said, glad he could finally get a word in edgewise. "We're taking care of it."

He was pretty sure that if Belinda Jones's eyebrows rose any higher, they'd climb straight off her face, but with a final look filled with the promise of a return trip if things didn't turn out to her utter satisfaction, the town busybody spun on one heel and sailed out of the squad room. He waited until the door closed in her wake before he turned to Sarah.

Standing there, in her uniform, her color high and her shoulders back, she'd never looked so sure of herself... and he'd never been more proud of her. He drew a breath and piped all his admiration into one long, low, "Wow!"

Sarah stared at the door for several seconds after the complaining citizen disappeared. Rocking back on her heels, she cast a quick look around the squad room. In a far corner, Sergeant Willis manned the phones. Though a pair of thick headphones protected them from being overheard, she motioned them to the other side of the room. "We need to talk." She gestured toward the door. "Outside."

Jake swallowed. In his limited experience, no good ever came from a conversation that started with, "we need to talk." He swallowed, and, bracing himself for bad news, stepped onto the sidewalk.

Sarah spun to face him. "Mrs. Jones is right, Jake," she began. "We have to do something. It's our duty to the people of this town. It's our job. Every day that goes by, there's something else that's fishy. Just tonight, her husband supposedly *died in the war*—"

"What's so *fishy* about that?" he blurted.

"But his name's not listed on the memorial? That's fishy," Sarah shot back.

"Who knows? Maybe he survived. She said he died at Malmedy. Not all the POWs were killed in the massacre. A few were taken in by the French Resistance. They stayed hidden and out of sight until the war ended."

Malmedy. The name had sounded so familiar when Hanna mentioned it in Dr. Lipscomb's office. Since then, he'd read everything he could get his hands on about the German massacre of U.S. prisoners near the end of the war. He stared down at Sarah. "What else? So, you're saying she's lying about the house? And the dog?" He took a breath. "The kennel is *named* after the dog she found. I mean, how could she have pulled that off?"

"She could have read the sign and then made up some story about some dog named Ruffin. Con artists think on their feet." Sarah sighed. "And the clothes, she could have found at some thrift store. And the license, she could've had printed. How can you keep wondering?"

"I'll tell you." His fingers touched the cool glass of the perfume bottle he'd slipped into his pocket after the lab report had come back this morning. "This," he said, holding up Hanna's vial of Lune de Paris.

"What? Her perfume? What does that have to do with anything?"

Accepting the challenge in Sarah's voice, he squared his shoulders. "Paris Moon. It was invented in 1928." He quoted the information he'd gleaned from the internet. "By the Forties, it was one of the most popular perfumes in the country."

"Okay, great. So… ?"

Dropping his voice, he let his tone grow more serious. "So, they stopped making it in the Sixties. There's no trace of it. I mean, there's no place she could have gotten this."

Sarah gave her big eyes an expressive roll. "She could have found an old bottle on eBay."

"The bottle, maybe. Not the perfume. I had the lab test it. According to the report they sent over, it hasn't oxidized yet. Even if the bottle had never been opened, there's no way it would still be good after seventy years. This is the real deal, Sarah."

He watched her closely, half expecting her to laugh out loud or, worse, call for the men in white coats. To her credit, she did neither, but stood, her weight shifting from one foot to another. Finally, a doubtful frown rippled across her face. She took the small vial he held out to her. For a long moment, she stared at it, considering.

He wanted to go on, wanted to tell her that he'd scoured the national databases for information about Hanna Morse and had drawn a blank. He wanted to fill Sarah in on the missing persons reports that proved not one single person in the entire country was looking for a thirty-three-year-old, blue-eyed blonde matching Hanna's description. But sensing he'd pushed Sarah as far as he could for one night, he kept those thoughts to himself. Later, there'd be time enough to fill her in on all the details. For now though, the situation called for a small dash of levity, and he grinned. "Hey, by the way… impressive whistle. Who taught you how to do that?"

"You did," Sarah admitted. "In the third grade."

Yes, indeed he had. When the older boys had picked on her, or her girlfriends had deserted her after a rare spat, he'd taught her that all she ever had to do was whistle, and he'd come running. When she was ten, she'd trusted him to be there for her, whenever she'd needed him. Now, he was asking her to trust him once more. To accept that, even though he couldn't explain how it happened, Hanna had somehow traveled through time to be with them.

He studied Sarah's face in the glow of light that came from the lamps over the entrance to the police station. The faint lines bracketing her mouth told him she'd chew on his theory until she made up her mind. But it was her eyes that caught his attention. Trust burned in her round blue orbs.

And for now, that was enough.

He resisted a sudden and unexpected urge to pull her into his arms and hold her close. Instead, he slung a friendly arm over her shoulders and said simply, "Let's go inside."

The rest, he decided, could come later.

Chapter Eight

*H*anna woke to the sounds of someone chopping wood just after sunrise. She looked out her window in time to see Jake make quick work of an armful of logs. His father, Mark, trudged by, carrying a large bag of salt. While she watched, the elder Stanton spread generous handfuls of the ice-melting crystals on sidewalks and steps. Moving away from the window, she stepped into another borrowed outfit and sped out of her room. She'd reached a decision during a long, sleepless night. Before the family headed off in different directions this morning, she wanted to share it with them.

In the big farm kitchen, she poured herself a cup of coffee from the pot that sat on its very own burner. Marveling at the smooth taste, she sipped the hot brew while she weighed her options. She'd never been much of a cook. She and Chet had been together such a short while that she'd never mastered the art of putting fluffy scrambled eggs, crisp bacon and sausage, and piping-hot pancakes on the table all at the same time. But in this new world she'd landed in, several modern conveniences made that job easier. Taking a long blue tube from a drawer in the refrigerator, she hoped that if she ever got home, she'd remember the magic of biscuits that came from a can.

By the time she'd peeled the dough apart and arranged it on a baking sheet, Jake's mother and sister had joined her and were busy adding their own contributions to the breakfast. With Gretchen in charge, sizzling bacon, scrambled eggs, and a massive stack of pancakes were added to the fare while Louise rounded out the meal with a huge bowl of freshly cut fruit. The good smells drew the entire family to the table. Hanna waited until the last strip of bacon had been eaten before she cleared her throat.

"I'd like to talk to everyone in a little while, if that'd be okay," she said.

Though her request met with a few curious looks, everyone agreed, and, not long after the dishes had been washed and the counters wiped down, the family gathered in the living room.

Standing before them, Hanna suppressed a sudden nervous energy by threading her fingers together. "First off, I want to apologize to everyone for being so blue last night," she started. "You all went out of your way to make the evening special, and I wanted you to know how much I appreciated it. The clothes. Caroling with you and your friends. It was all so wonderful. And it made me stop and think how much I really have to be grateful for."

She took a big breath to steady her nerves. The next part was hard to talk about, even for her. "The truth is, I don't know how I got here. And… and I don't know how I'll ever get home. This whole thing is as surreal to me as it must be for all of you." Really, when she stopped to consider how strange her appearance and actions must seem to everyone, she imagined that it had taken some kind of miracle for Jake and his family to let her stay with them at all.

"And yet… you've all been so kind to me. So, so kind." She stopped to survey the room. When Jake brought her to his family's farm, she'd worried that Louise would always doubt her story, but over the last week, every trace of suspicion had faded from the young mother's face. Beside her mom, Gwennie gazed at her with the complete acceptance that only the very young and very old possessed. Hanna gave the little girl a special smile before she moved on to Jake's parents. From the very start, Mark and Gretchen had gone out of their way to make her feel welcome in their home. She'd never be able to thank them enough for all they'd done for her. But the man she owed the most to, the man responsible for her being here as opposed to sitting in a darkened cell somewhere, stood before the fireplace. Jake's unquestioning belief in her had seen her through more dark moments than she wanted to count.

A lump formed in her throat. She swallowed past

it. "Just last week, when I was back—" *Back… where? Back… when?* "—back in real time, I told Dottie, right there in front of the movie house, I told her, 'Nothing ever gets solved by blubbering.' It just doesn't do anyone any good at all. Well, I forgot that for a while since I've been here. But from now on out, I'm going to take those words to heart. And since I don't think I'll ever be able to go home again, I'm going to make the best of things here. I'm going to find happiness. Going to find some way to be useful. And stop wishing things would be… different."

She wasn't sure how she'd fit in to this new world, but she'd never been a quitter. Hadn't she put herself through nursing school when so many of her friends had taken jobs in factories or sold papers on street corners? It had been tough, making Chet's paycheck stretch far enough to cover her tuition and books, as well as the mortgage on their house. But she'd done it. She'd earned her nursing pin, found a job she loved doing, and even built up a little nest egg.

She wasn't about to give up now just because things weren't the same as they'd always been. No matter what else had changed, her determination to make the best of things hadn't. The least she could do to honor her husband's memory was to figure out how to adjust to a world in which car trunks opened on their own, people talked on phones that didn't need wires, and biscuits came from a tube.

A sense of purpose swelled in her chest. She thrust her fingers into the pocket of the slim-fitting black pants Louise had loaned her and pulled out the key that had fallen from her coat pocket as she'd been getting ready for bed last night. Less than a week ago in real time—her time—the key had been shiny and new when Charlie had pressed it into her hand. Now tarnished and dull, it dangled from the chain she held up for everyone to see.

"I may have a solution for the town's Christmas lights. The ones for the gazebo. It's not going to change the world, but it's something."

It was a start, a step toward acceptance, toward finding her purpose in this new and modern world.

Surveying the rows of books and the checkout desk at the library, Hanna felt so unsure of herself that her knees practically knocked together. It was all well and good to think about finding one's purpose, but to do it under the watchful gaze of so many pairs of suspicion-filled eyes, well, that was something else altogether. Her stomach churned as she looked out over the crowd that had gathered in the library.

She wished Gretchen and Mark had been able to join them, but her staunchest supporters had stayed at the farm, where the daily chores couldn't be ignored. Much as she adored Gwennie, how much help could a little girl be? As oblivious to the drama unfolding around her as an any eight-year-old, Gwen paged through a book from the children's section while Louise hovered over her child like a mother who feared her daughter's faith was about to be shattered. Meanwhile, all black leather and stern expressions, Jake and Sarah had taken up positions at the edge of the group. Jake had introduced Belinda Jones as a concerned citizen, but the woman apparently saw herself as the judge between right and wrong in Central Falls. She stood, her hip cocked and lips pressed together, looking for all the world like a predator waiting to pounce on her prey at the slightest sign of weakness.

"One of the nurses' stations, it was right there, I think." Hanna's voice trembled despite her best efforts. She scanned the section of the library where they stood. Where were the walls that had separated the nurses' station from the patient wards? Baffled by the sweeping changes that had taken place since she'd last stepped foot in the hospital, she did her best to explain. "It all looks so different now. And, well, the adult patients' ward was upstairs. And my favorite one, the pediatrics, it was over in that corner." That much she knew for sure. "There was a door over there." She pointed to one wall. "It went to the back stairwell."

How many times had she trudged up and down the staircase, fetching another divider to place between beds or toting patient records to the basement, where they were stored after discharge? Too many to count. But where was it now?

She eyed the tall bookcases that hadn't been there when the building had been a hospital. Had someone plastered over the door? Surely they wouldn't. She had to be mistaken. Her confusion growing, she crossed to the seating area on the other side of the room. "Or, maybe it was over here?"

Gwen finished with the book she'd been reading. Sticking it on the bookshelf, she reached for another one. "Hey," she called. "There's a door here." She pushed aside several children's books.

"There is?" Hanna spun. There was! Though the shiny brass knob had lost its luster, the hardware hadn't changed a bit. She eyed the shelves. If she squinted just right, she could see the outline of the jamb above the highest one. "Can we move this bookcase?"

"Sure we can." Louise jumped into action, taking an armful of books and toting them to a nearby table. With Gwennie's help, they made quick work of the task. Once the shelves were bare, Jake stepped forward. He grasped the heavy bookcase and slid it aside to reveal the wooden door behind it.

A quiver of excitement rippled through Hanna. "That goes down to the storage room." She was certain of it. She tugged the door open. She gasped as a burst of stale, cold air rose from an area that had been closed off for who knew how long.

"Come on, it's this way," she said. Unwilling to wait another second now that—finally—something felt familiar, and, in an odd sense, hers, she ducked under the cobwebs industrious spiders had spun at the top of the door frame.

The others weren't so certain and lingered in the library.

"Are you sure?" Her driving gloves clutched in one

hand, Mrs. Jones refused to cross the threshold until Jake brushed away the spider webs and started down the stairs in front of her.

"I can't believe we never knew this was down here." Sarah whispered loud enough to be heard above the noise her boots made on the bare wooden steps.

Her confidence growing with every step, Hanna chose to ignore the doubts the others raised and led the way down the winding, narrow staircase. Behind her, Louise cautioned her daughter to stay close, but the young mother might as well have saved her breath. Determined not to miss out, Gwen raced down the stairs on Hanna's heels. Together, they rounded the last corner and entered the storage room.

The thick layer of dust that coated boxes of patient records—and everything else—dismayed Hanna. When the building had been a hospital, everything had been kept clean as a whistle, even the storage closets. If their head nurse saw the jumbled pile of bed frames that stood in the corner now, or the curtained screens that had been stacked slapdash against a storage locker, she'd have something to say about the mess, for sure.

But bed frames weren't exactly what Hanna had come here to find.

"There, behind those." With a strength she didn't know she possessed, she muscled the heavy room dividers out of her way. Removing the key from her pocket, she took a breath. This was it, the moment of truth. The Christmas decorations were her only proof that she'd somehow been transported into the future. If they weren't here…

She let the thought trail off. The decorations *had* to be in the locker. She slipped the key into the hole. Her thoughts stuttered when it held fast. She fought an urge to slap her palm to her head. Of course the door wouldn't open right away. After all this time, the lock had probably rusted shut. Her heart pounding, she twisted the key, first one way and then the other.

Snap!

The lock sprang. The knob twisted in her hand. With a loud squeak, the door swung open on rusty hinges. An oversized Christmas ornament tumbled from the top of a haphazard pile of decorations. The purple globe landed in her outstretched hand while a chorus of *oohs* and *aahs* sounded from behind her.

"Wow!" Louise gasped. "Look at all those."

"There should be enough in here to decorate the entire gazebo." Hanna grabbed a crate of multi-colored bulbs that hung from thick strands of wire. Other than a little dust, they looked none the worse for wear after so many years. Setting the box aside, she reached for the next one. A few shreds of tissue paper clung to the glass ornaments that had been carefully wrapped and stored away more than seventy years ago. She paused, mesmerized by colored glass that, even to her eyes, looked quaint and old-fashioned compared to the decorations she'd seen around town the last few days.

How had so much time passed so quickly?

"Well, well, well. I always wondered what was in that locker."

A voice she didn't recognize broke Hanna's spell. Turning away from the closet, she summoned up a smile for a white-haired gentleman who'd entered the storage room. The low buzz of conversation died when, like Moses at the Red Sea, he cut a path through the group. Only, instead of heading for the Promised Land, he walked straight toward her.

"It's nice to see you again," he said in a tone reserved for Sunday morning church services.

She squinted to get a better look at him. Fashionable clothes and a regal bearing identified him as someone important, someone well-respected within Central Falls. But she'd never seen his lined face before. And though there was just a hint of something familiar about his eyes, she was reasonably certain they'd never met. At least, not within the last few days.

"I'm sorry," she apologized, not wanting to appear rude. "Do I know you?"

"It's Mr. Cook," Gwennie blurted. The little girl giggled. "He's the man I told you about. He's the one who made this building into the library."

"Oh!" Hanna bit her lower lip. Careful not to break any of them, she returned the box of ornaments to the closet. "Then, you must think I'm trespassing. But I can explain—"

"My dear, you don't have to explain a thing. Somehow, over the years, people lost track of the keys to that old locker. I can't tell you how happy it makes me to know that you had one." Mr. Cook scoured the room with an appraising glance. "Tell you what, it's far too dusty and dirty for women and children down here. Let me have my assistant bring some workers in. They'll have everything cleaned up in no time. And when they're finished, they'll take the decorations to the gazebo." His eyes narrowed as he turned to Mrs. Jones. "I bet you could find enough volunteers to string the lights and hang all the ornaments this afternoon, couldn't you?"

"Um, um. Of course! In fact—" After a moment of fluster, Belinda Jones preened at being singled out for the task by the town's leading citizen. She snatched her cell phone from her purse. By the time her heels clattered on the wooden stairs, she was already marshalling her troops. "Yes, Harv, that's what I said. The gazebo. Grab everyone you can and—"

The door at the top of the stairs closed, shutting off Belinda's voice.

Mr. Cook rubbed age-spotted hands together. "There, that'll keep her busy and out of our hair for a few hours. I never was much good at putting up with people who insist on butting their noses in where they don't belong." His sheepish grin brought smiles to everyone's faces. "Now, if you wouldn't mind, I'd like to show you something at my house. It won't take long."

A frown tugged on Hanna's lips. Though she felt oddly at ease around Mr. Cook, and everyone in the room treated him with deference and respect, she couldn't simply go off with a man she didn't know. It wouldn't be proper.

As if he sensed her discomfort, Jake cleared his throat. "If you don't mind, sir, I'll come along, too."

Hanna swung a hopeful glance at Mr. Cook. Though she half expected him to object, the older gentleman clapped his hands. "Why, yes, that would be wonderful. In fact, why don't you all come? You're more than welcome." The smile lines bracketing his mouth deepened. "I think we could rustle up some tea for the adults and hot cocoa for your little girl here." He nodded at Louise. "There might even be cookies."

"Can we?" Gwen tipped her head to look at her mother. "Can we go?"

Though the idea held obvious appeal, Louise shook her head. "Thank you so much, but I promised my mom and dad we wouldn't be long." Placing a hand on her daughter's shoulder, Louise leaned over Gwennie. "You can tell Gram and Pops what Hanna found. They'll be very excited."

"They will, won't they?" Gwen's eyes sparkled with an eagerness that outweighed even hot chocolate and cookies.

Mr. Cook turned to Sarah next. "How about you, then, officer?"

Though Hanna hoped for the chance to get to know Jake's partner better, the slim young woman shook her head. "I have to get back to the station. Chief Munson will want a full report."

"Another time, then." Mr. Cook nodded as if he'd

expected her answer. With gestures courtly enough for a state event, he guided the group out of the storage area.

At the doorway, Hanna stopped to give the boxes of Christmas decorations a last, lingering glance. A longing so deep it hurt to breathe stirred in her chest.

Hanna Morse, you stop that right now.

It was silly for her to wish she could go back in time to 1945. After all, it wasn't as if she had a lot to go back to. Oh, she'd been happy there once. When Chet had been alive, when she'd planned on making a happy home for him and for their children, then she'd looked forward to the lives they'd lead. But without Chet, what was there to return to?

She swallowed, hard, and pushed the pain away. Like the ornaments she'd discovered in the locker, the ones that would now bring joy and happiness to a new generation, she needed to straighten up and find her own purpose in this strange world she'd somehow landed in. Wondering what on earth Mr. Cook could possibly have to show her, she headed up the stairs behind the others.

Chapter Nine

*H*anna fought to keep her jaw from coming unhinged as she followed Mr. Cook through the foyer with its glossy marble floor to the living room where a cheery fire burned in a massive stone fireplace. She managed, just barely, but knew she must look like a kid in a candy store. She eyed a towering Christmas tree decorated with ornaments that had been antiques, even in her own time. Everywhere she looked, knickknacks and mementos from their host's travels around the globe crowded the tops of sturdy tables covered with lace doilies. Framed photographs of their host in places she recognized, but with people she didn't, dotted the walls. Glad she wasn't the only one who felt a bit overwhelmed, she traded wide-eyed glances with Jake when she caught the deputy studying a replica of the Eiffel Tower.

Did he want to visit there? Had he already been?

She realized how little she really knew about Jake,

but tucked her questions away for later when Mr. Cook opened the wide double doors to his study. The restraint she'd held in check wavered. It failed completely when she stepped into a room where row upon row of books lined floor-to-ceiling shelves. Rich leather seating, ottomans, and glass-domed lights created perfect spots to indulge in a love of reading. Unable to resist, she trailed her fingertips along the spines of a row of leather-bound books.

"Books, as you can see, are my passion." Mr. Cook's expression softened as he gazed at the volumes that crowded his shelves. He straightened one, moved another to a different spot. "That's why I saved the old hospital. They were going to tear that thing down. Can you believe that?"

"Tear it down?" Wasn't the building brand new? Hanna stopped herself before she could ask the foolish question. The hospital, which had seemed so modern to her, had been built three-quarters of a century ago. She swallowed. "It makes a perfect library," she conceded.

"Books saved me from a very lonely youth, being a child of the war and all."

From the way Mr. Cook peered at her, she thought he'd expected the statement to cause a stir. The silence that descended on the room stretched out while he stared at her and waited. She wracked her brain, trying to come up with an appropriate response. Unable to find one, she gave him her most polite nod. The war had made orphans of so many people, she wasn't sure why he'd think his situation was so different from the others'.

"Sometimes it's the smallest things that change a life. For me, it was reading." As if lost in pleasant memories of the past, Mr. Cook didn't say anything else for a long beat. When his focus finally cleared, he gave a sheepish grin like someone who'd been caught napping. He cleared his throat. "I've asked my assistant to bring tea," he announced.

Within moments, a slender redhead entered the room. A pair of young golden retrievers bounded into the library along with him. Their bushy tails wagging, the dogs nipped at the young man's heels. Their paws skidded and slipped on the polished hardwood floors. Worried that the frolicking dogs would cause Mr. Cook's assistant to lose his grip on the heavy tray, Hanna traded concerned glances with Jake.

Should we offer to help?

But their host didn't seem at all worried. He stood warming himself by the fire, his hands clasped behind his back while his aide lowered the tray to a nearby table without incident.

"Somehow Julius manages to never spill a drop, despite these incorrigible dogs of mine."

At Mr. Cook's praise, Julius's ears pinked. He snapped his fingers, and the dogs followed him out of the room.

"Would you like tea?" Mr. Cook lifted an ornate china pot.

Hints of jasmine and orange wafted from the cup

Hanna took from their host. Though she enjoyed visiting his elegant home, she couldn't help but wonder why he'd invited her here. What did he want to show her? She'd barely taken a sip of her tea when he squinted at her over the rim of his own cup.

"I have to be truthful here." Mr. Cook's expression resembled that of a boy who'd gotten caught with his hand in the cookie jar. "I've heard all the stories about you and… time travel."

"Oh!" Her cup rattled into the saucer when she lost her grip on the handle. For some reason, she'd expected more than simple curiosity from a man so well-respected in Central Falls. Not afraid to let her disappointment show, she scolded him like she would a patient who'd failed to follow the doctor's orders. "Oh, so you just wanted to see the talk of the town."

"That's true, but…" Mr. Cook set his tea aside. He paused as if uncertain how to continue. "Actually, I wanted to see how you're doing."

Perplexed, she searched his face. The reassurance she saw in his straightforward gaze sparked a tiny hope. "Do you mean that… ? Do you mean that you believe me?"

Blue eyes twinkling, the older man chortled. "Oh, more than that." Moving to the mantel, he said, "I have something that belongs to you. It's from a long time ago." With a tender smile, he took a black box from the shelf and placed it in her hands.

Looking down, she suddenly couldn't catch her breath. "It's a camera," she managed in a strangled voice. One that looked strangely familiar. Quickly, she flipped it over and studied the corner. Her initials gleamed against the soft, black leather, just as they'd done the day Chet had carved them in the case. "That's *my* camera," she gasped. Her husband had given it to her as a going-away present the day he'd left to go overseas. Tears welled in her eyes. Scrubbing at them, she felt her mouth gape open. She closed it enough to ask, "How did you get it?"

"Well, now…" Silence as thick as hand-churned butter filled the room as the older man's watery blue eyes met hers. "Nurse Hanna," he said softly. "I'm Toby."

"Toby? But…" How could that be? Toby was a young boy. Less than a week ago, he'd been a patient recuperating from a bad fall.

Boneless, her knees bent beneath her. She sank onto the leather couch. She studied the face of their host. She skimmed past the deep creases around his mouth to his wrinkled neck, noted the slight bend in his posture, the shock of thick, white hair. How could this grown man be Toby?

Mr. Cook's wizened eyes met hers. "It's true." He nodded.

"But you were just a little boy, and now you're…" Why, the man had to be in his eighties if he was a day.

Words, like her legs, failed her. Her thoughts tumbled over one another. Ever since she'd climbed out of the window of the storage shed, she'd half convinced herself that this was all a dream. But it wasn't, was it?

The ornaments they'd found at the library proved she'd traveled into the future. The solidity of the camera in her hands offered further evidence.

Now, Toby was…

The truth sank in. The boy from her past had shown up in her present. She might not have any idea of how she'd gotten here—to this time, to this place—but she finally had proof that she'd been telling the truth all along. Excitement raced through her. She turned to Jake. "Why, I used to read to him. When he was a little boy."

Though the deputy's eyes grew to the size of saucers, he didn't say a word. Not that she faulted him for that. Honestly, what was there to say? She'd been a young woman when she'd last seen Toby. Now, here he was, an aged figure of a man, while she looked exactly the same.

"A lot of years have passed since then, Nurse Hanna." With a slight groan, Mr. Cook sat down beside her.

"Oh, your arm!" she blurted. "It healed!"

"That happened so long ago, I'd almost forgotten why I was in the hospital." Chuckling, Toby twisted his arm from the right to the left and back again. "Good as new," he declared even as tears spilled from his eyes. When they ran down his cheeks, he snagged a napkin from the tea tray and blotted them. "Look at you!" His voice filled with awe. "So young."

"And you're not a little boy anymore. Oh!" She clamped a hand over her mouth. "I'm staring. That's rude, and I don't mean to be. It's just, I'm sorry but, but there's so much I don't understand. I want to know… everything. My head is bursting with so many questions, I don't even know where to start."

As if they sensed the excitement in the air and didn't want to be left out, Toby's two dogs bounded into the room. Their nails clicked against the hardwood floors in a series of rapid-fire bursts when the retrievers chased one another around the Christmas tree. Their playful barks drowned out the conversation.

"Hey, stop that." Shaking his head and laughing, Toby turned to the dogs. "Ralph! Rex!" he called, his love for them apparent in his good-natured tone. "Both of you, stop." The dogs skidded to a halt in front of him as Toby reached into his sweater pocket. After pulling out a handful of doggie treats, he gave one to each of the pups. "Okay, now. Be good boys and go on." With a slight jerk of his head, he sent the pair off to another part of the house. "I'm sorry about the boys," Toby said once the dogs raced out of the room. "My sister breeds them. It's become a family business." He faced her again. His expression softening, he reached for her hand. "Actually, because of you."

"Me?" What could she possibly have to do with it? Between her job at the hospital and all the responsibilities of her house and car, she hadn't even had time to own a cat.

"Yes." A new awareness burned in Toby's blue eyes. "You remember when you took the lost dog home?"

"The night of the storm." She nodded. How could she forget? It had led to the strangest experience of her life.

"The owner was so grateful that she came to the hospital to thank you the next day."

Why didn't she remember that? "Oh!" she gasped. "But I wasn't there. I was…" She brushed a hand through her hair. She'd been so caught up in her own predicament that she hadn't stopped to consider how her friends, her coworkers, had reacted. "I guess I was gone."

Toby threaded his fingers through hers. "Your disappearance created quite a stir. They searched for days. When there was no trace of you, someone said you must have simply run off to start a new life. But I knew different. I always knew you wouldn't leave without saying goodbye."

"Never in a million years." She squeezed Toby's hand. She'd never been one to run away from her problems, but in this case, she'd had no choice in the matter.

The ghost of the little boy she'd once known showed in Toby's knowing smile. "Anyway, when Sue Bunce showed up at the hospital to thank you for returning her dog, someone told her if she really wanted to return the favor, she should come up and read to me." His smile widened. "Because *I*—he tapped his chest—"I was your favorite boy in the hospital."

"You were," she admitted with a laugh. The head nurse would've read her the riot act over that—nurses were trained to give everyone fair and equal treatment. They weren't supposed to have favorites. But right from the start, she'd known Toby was special. They'd had such good times, reading and whispering stories to one another while the other children in the ward napped or visited with their families. Lost in thought, she tapped her finger against her chin. "The nurse who spoke with Mrs. Bunce—that must have been Julia. Or Dottie." The two women had been her best friends. She could only imagine how worried they'd been when she hadn't shown up for work or when she'd disappeared without leaving so much as a note.

Toby leaned back until his head rested on the leather seat. "And then, the nurse mentioned that you were hoping that I wouldn't have to spend Christmas alone."

"Oh, it was definitely Dottie." She hadn't told anyone else about her call to the orphanage.

"Yeah." Toby's gaze intensified. He leaned forward, his attention honing in on her. "So the Bunces took me home."

"Oh, how wonderful!" Her heart swelled until she thought it might burst out of her chest. Though she hadn't been there herself, her friend had followed through on her promise to see that Toby didn't spend the holiday at the orphanage. Closing her eyes, she imagined Toby's surprise when he came down the stairs at the Bunces' house on Christmas morning. Sue and Hal had been so nice to her, she just bet they'd created an extra-special Christmas for the boy and—"Oh, yes. I remember! They had a little child."

"Clara." The years fell away from Toby's face as he mentioned the name. "My sister."

"Your sister?" How was that even possible? She stilled. Shouldn't she know by now that *nothing* was impossible?

"The Bunces adopted me."

A surprised gasp escaped her lips. Toby's Christmas visit had turned out even better than she'd dared hope for. She pressed one hand to her chest.

"And Sue, my adopted mother, realized how important Ruffin was to the family," Toby went on, "so she started a kennel. And then, after seeing how much help Ruffin was to Dad—he lost his sight when I was still in my teens—she began training him and his offspring as guide dogs."

Pieces of the puzzle began to fit into place. "That's why I keep seeing so many golden retrievers in Central Falls now."

"Yes." Toby nodded agreeably. "They're service dogs. They've helped a lot of people over the years."

The young pups chose that moment to race back into the room. This time, instead of reaching for a handful of treats, their owner merely shook his head. "So, those two are dropouts. C'mere, Ralph, Rex." Toby patted his knee. When the dogs ignored him and kept chasing each other's tails, he kneeled on the floor. Instantly, they ran over and nosed his pockets. He laughed. "They're too silly to be service dogs. So they're mine." His movements good-natured and kind, he ruffled their fur.

When Ralph and Rex responded by covering Toby's face with slobbery kisses, Hanna grabbed her camera. Hoping to capture the moment, she only snapped one picture before she realized that she'd reached the end of the roll. "Oh, darn," she said. "I'm out of film."

"Film." Jake whistled, low and long. "No one uses that anymore," he informed her while she twisted the knob to eject the metal canister from the camera. "These days, everything's digital."

"What?" Was this another thing she'd have to learn about, like telephones that fit in the palm of your hand?

"That's all right." Toby spoke with all the reassurance of someone who'd experienced a lifetime of changes. He hadn't had them all thrust at him at once, but there must have been times when he, too, had despaired of ever keeping up with technology. "I know someone who can develop that for you. There's a little shop down on Main that still processes film on request."

With a sigh, she placed the canister in his outstretched hand. Wishing something—anything—had stayed the same as what she remembered, she glanced at Toby. There were so many things she wanted to know, questions he might be able to answer. Had all their boys finally come home from the war? What had happened to Chet's name on the memorial? Had Frank and Julia gotten married? Why didn't people nowadays celebrate all the traditions that had made Christmas so special?

Slow down. One question at a time.

She studied Toby's face, searching for signs of the little boy she'd once known. Deep lines bracketed his mouth and fanned out over his cheeks. Wrinkles crisscrossed his forehead. Loose, sagging skin covered the backs of his hands. He'd been a youngster, not even in his teens, when they'd known each other... before. If he'd aged this much, what had happened to her friends, her coworkers? She gulped, and, bracing herself for bad news, asked, "And Dottie? How did her life turn out?"

"Ah, Dottie." Toby's expression turned pensive. "She's still here."

Shock sent little ripples of excitement down her spine. "She... she's alive?"

A shadow passed over Toby's face. "She is. Her memory's not what it used to be, and she has to use a wheelchair, but I keep in touch. She lives in an assisted living facility on the edge of town. It's, uh"—he straightened the collar of his sweater—"I assure you, it's a very nice place."

She gave the older gentleman a studied look. "You've done so much for Central Falls. You opened the library. You sponsor the science fair. I bet you're helping Dottie, too, aren't you?" When Toby answered with a shrug, she went on. "What prompted you to give back, to lend a hand to those whose lives didn't turn out as good as yours?"

"Ah, Nurse Hanna." Toby's smile deepened. "The other boys in the orphanage with me, their lives followed a different path from mine. A few of them ran away when they were still in their teens. The ones that stayed, they didn't go to college. Most dropped out of school before they graduated. They ended up taking whatever jobs they could find."

Hanna took a deep breath. She'd heard people say that the orphanage did little more than warehouse the children until they were old enough to be put to work. That was one of the reasons she'd wanted so badly to help Toby spend Christmas somewhere else.

"I was one of the lucky ones," Toby said as he patted her hand. "I didn't know it at the time, but landing in the hospital was the best thing that ever happened to me because that's where I met you. And because of you, I was adopted. And that opened up a whole new world of possibilities for me. Right from the start, my new mom and dad treated me like their very own son. They made sure I went to school, had nice clothes to wear, and had plenty to eat. And things turned out very good for me." He gestured toward the beautiful furnishings that filled his lovely home. "Along the way, I've always tried to make a difference in people's lives, like you—and Dottie—did in mine. Now that she needs a little help, I make sure she's well cared for. It's another way I can make a difference."

When he paused, Hanna pressed her hands over her heart. Though Toby thought she'd changed his life, she knew the truth—she hadn't done anything nearly as grand as he had.

Toby straightened as if a new idea had just occurred to him. A teasing glint came into his blue eyes. "Speaking of Dottie, would you like to see her?"

The world slowed. Would she? "Yes!"

Okay, she might have bounced on the couch a little. That was something Gwennie would do, and not the ladylike response someone as wealthy and refined as Toby would expect. She calmed herself. She couldn't get her hopes up. Dottie had celebrated her thirtieth birthday a few days after Thanksgiving. But, unlike Hanna's own fast-forward into the future, her friend had lived her life in this time. Like Toby, she'd aged. She might even be infirm.

"How, how is she, really?" Hanna asked.

Toby nodded as if he'd expected the question. "It varies. She has her good days and her bad ones. We'll hope this is a good day."

"But she's here. Dottie's here." No matter what, she had to see the woman who'd seen her through some of the worst—and the best—days of her life. "And we can see her. Today."

"If you'd like." Toby ran his fingers through Ralph's fur.

"Yes, please," she repeated, tamping down her enthusiasm until it bubbled beneath the surface. Eager to be off, she scanned Toby's face. "How soon can we go?"

Chapter Ten

Jake took his time driving through Central Falls's quiet streets while, in the back seat, Tobias and Hanna chatted away like two magpies on a tree branch. He smiled to himself. His passengers had been talking nonstop ever since they'd piled into the car. Their topics had no rhyme or reason but bounced from presidents to television shows like balls scattering out of the rack on a pool table. Now, Tobias was filling her in on what it had been like for him to go from being an orphan with no prospects, to a beloved son who had the world as his oyster. The only fly in the proverbial ointment had been his sister Clara, who, apparently, had been less than pleased to give up her status as an only child or to share her parents' affections with a complete stranger. Fortunately for both of them, Tobias had found a way to get on her good side.

"Yeah, Clara was about six or seven, and she hated spiders. She'd run screaming from the room if she even saw a spiderweb. But that day—I can remember it like it was yesterday—that day, spiders had hatched in the field Mom used for her training exercises. Clara's job was to groom the dogs afterward. Well, she was brushing Ruffin when she discovered thousands of tiny, baby spiders clinging to the dog's fur. The screams that rang through the house that day—let me tell you." The old man laughed out loud.

"Oh, my goodness!" Hanna exclaimed. "What did she do?"

"It wasn't what she did, my dear. It was what I did. I grabbed the nearest hose and went to work bathing that dog. I scrubbed him down three times, went through an entire bottle of doggie shampoo. But that wasn't the worst part. Do you have any idea how much hair a retriever has? I spent hours sifting through it all with a fine-toothed comb. But it was worth it. Clara was my friend for life after that. We talk on the phone or see each other every day."

"Oh, I'm so glad everything turned out well for you, Toby. You were such a smart little boy. I always thought you deserved all the best."

"We're almost there," Jake announced. In the rearview mirror, he glimpsed the happiness that shone in Hanna's eyes. Glad for his part in putting it there, he let his smile widen.

Arriving at the next intersection, he turned off the main road onto a tree-lined drive. At the end, electric candles glowed in every window of a stately, two-story building. Every trace of ice and snow had been removed from sidewalks and stairs that led to doors decorated with wreaths and colored lights. The atmosphere gave off a clean, welcoming vibe, and he nodded. This was just the kind of place he'd expect Tobias to provide for Hanna's friend.

Inside, he hung back as staff members greeted the older gentleman with the kind of familiarity reserved for frequent visitors. Within minutes, they set off behind a young nurse who led them down the wide, carpeted hallway toward a curving staircase at the end of the building. Rooms opened onto the corridor. Most of the doors were closed, but a buzz of conversation came from one of them. As he passed, Jake stole a peek through the open door. He smiled at a bevy of well-dressed senior citizens who furiously dabbed colored strips of paper whenever the woman up front called a new number.

"Bingo!" a voice trilled.

Wishing them all a silent good luck, he hurried after the rest of his party, who'd walked straight past the elevator and were now halfway up the staircase.

"I heard she was quite the character once," the nurse said as he reached the rest of the group.

"That's Dottie," Hanna agreed with a laugh.

At the second-floor landing, the nurse sobered. "I have to warn you that since I've been here, she doesn't talk a lot. I'm not sure how much she remembers."

The nurse rapped twice beneath a colorful tinsel wreath that had been hung on the door closest to the elevator. Without waiting for an answer, she led them into a spacious, well-designed suite. They'd decided earlier that it'd be better to let Tobias greet Dottie first, so Jake lingered in the small foyer with Hanna while the older gentleman crossed to a figure seated in a wheelchair.

While Tobias spoke with Dottie, Jake took in the details of the room. A thick Oriental carpet sat atop glossy hardwood floors. Heavy drapes hung at the windows. Books which, judging from their leather bindings, had come from Tobias' library were stacked on a nightstand that had been strategically placed near the window. Christmas cards, letters, and curios dotted a low mantel. White lights twinkled from a tabletop tree decorated with silver balls that reflected the fake flames from an electric fireplace.

His circuit of the room complete, his gaze landed on Hanna. She'd paled under her blond hair, and he cleared his throat to draw her attention. "You okay?"

Her sad smile told him she wasn't. "I've missed out on so much."

He gave her hand a sympathetic squeeze. "It'll be all right. Everything will work out just the way it's supposed to. You'll see."

"Will it?" Her breath shuddered. "I know I said I was done feeling sorry for myself, that I was going to make the best of this new life... but how am I supposed to do that when everyone I've ever known is either gone or—" Her words stumbled to a halt. "Or like Dottie?"

Much as he hated to agree with her, Hanna had

raised a good point. Though Dottie's hair gleamed silver in the afternoon light that streamed through the window, though a strand of pearls graced the loose flesh of her neck and small diamonds sparkled at her earlobes, she hadn't moved or said a word since they walked into the room. How would she react when she saw Hanna? Would she recognize her friend? Would she realize that Hanna hadn't aged a day since the last time they'd seen each other?

He shook his head. Time travel, who would have thought it was even possible? He'd been so busy coming to grips with the possibility that Hanna had magically leap-frogged more than seventy years into the future that he hadn't stopped to consider how hard this was on her. To wake up one day and find out that everything had changed and nothing was the same—he couldn't imagine how he'd begin deal with the sudden change if he'd been the one to show up in her time instead of the other way around. No wonder she'd half convinced herself that she was living out some kind of dream, a dream that had turned into reality when she'd come face-to-face with Tobias.

"Let's just see how it goes," he suggested. "One thing I do know is that you're far stronger than you give yourself credit for. I know you can do this. And with my help, and Toby's, you won't have to do it alone."

"Thank you, Jake." Hanna took another shuddery breath. "That means a lot." She nodded to the pair at the window. "I wonder what he's saying to her."

"He's probably reminiscing about the good old days. Reminding her of all the fun the two of you used to have together." At least, that was what he'd be doing if he were the one kneeling beside Dottie's wheelchair. He stuck his hands in his pockets and propped one shoulder against the wall.

As if he'd heard their whispered conversation, Tobias glanced toward them. "Dottie," he said, raising his voice, "Nurse Hanna is here to see you."

Tobias's smile wavered the tiniest bit when Dottie simply continued to stare out the window, her eyes unfocused and unseeing. He tried again. "Nurse Hanna?" he said, louder this time. "She's come to visit you."

Dottie didn't so much as twitch a muscle.

Slowly, Tobias stood. With a slight shake of his head, he let everyone know that this was not one of Dottie's better days. "You want to try, Hanna?"

Though Hanna summoned a broad smile, Jake read the sorrow in her hesitant steps when she moved across the room. His heart went out to her. It occurred to him that any force strong enough to move a person across time ought to be able to help in this situation, too. Crossing his fingers, he wished for a tiny miracle as she sank to her knees in front of her friend.

"Oh, Dottie... look at you!" Hanna ran her fingers through the elderly woman's silver curls, straightened the lacy red shawl around her thin, stooped shoulders. "You're so beautiful. Same as always. I know it's been a long time, but do you remember me? It's me, Hanna," she said with a catch in her voice.

Jake didn't think he'd ever wished so hard for a response as he did right then, but Dottie didn't move. No smile graced her lips. Her gaze remained fixed on some distant spot beyond the window pane.

A pleading look filled the blue eyes Hanna turned on the nurse who stood nearby. "Can she hear?"

"Her doctors say she can," the young woman answered softly. "But she doesn't respond to much anymore."

Like Jake had noticed her doing before whenever she faced a puzzle she couldn't quite figure out, Hanna nibbled on her lower lip. After a long minute, determination flashed across her face, and she squared her shoulders. He watched her take a deep breath and try again.

"Dottie, it's me, Hanna." A new, deeper intensity turned her eyes a brilliant blue. "Dottie, can you hear me? It's me, Hanna."

He had to give it to her—she was a determined soul. How she managed to hold onto that bright smile when Dottie didn't so much as look her way, he'd never know. But she did. He wasn't quite sure how long she sat there, stroking Dottie's hand and calling out to her. He only knew he'd have given up long before she did. And that would have been a shame because, at last, Dottie's focus shifted to her friend. Her vision cleared until she homed in on Hanna as if she were a lighthouse and Dottie was a ship badly in need of a port. After a long moment, recognition flared in the older woman's wide brown eyes. Her mouth worked.

"Oh!" Tears spilled down Hanna's cheeks. "She's trying to say something."

Like someone speaking with a mouthful of marbles, Dottie uttered a single unintelligible word.

"I didn't get that, Dottie. Can you say it again?" Hanna leaned forward.

"Commmmm…" Dottie mouthed. Frustration glinted in her eyes. "Commmmennnnt."

"What?" Hanna took both of her friend's hands in her own. "Comment on what?"

But like a lantern that had run out of fuel, Dottie only gave a sad smile. Before anyone in the room could react, the life went out of her eyes. A huge sigh escaped through her lips, and her shoulders slumped.

"Dottie?" Hanna called. "Dottie?"

But it was no use. The elderly woman had retreated into her earlier stupor.

While Hanna tried again and again to get a response, Jake straightened. In slow, deliberate stages, he shook off the tension that had built in his chest during Hanna's too-short exchange with her friend. Clearly, Dottie had been trying to convey an important message, but what? Was there a clue somewhere in her room?

He crossed to the mantel, where some caring soul had arranged the resident's Christmas cards and letters. Picking them up one by one, he searched for anything out of the ordinary. He'd almost reached the last of them when his attention fell to a sepia-toned postcard from a long-ago era. On one side, above a town that looked very much like Central Falls, a bright light blazed a trail across the night sky. He flipped the card over to read the note, and his pulse jumped.

He swallowed and read the card a second time.

"Um, Hanna?" Surprised that his voice sounded so calm, and, well, normal under the circumstances, he crooked a finger at the young woman. "Hanna. You should see this." His determination wavered a little when Hanna pinned him with an annoyed grimace. But knowing what he'd found changed everything, he persisted. "Seriously. You need to see this. Now."

"What do you have there, Jake?"

Tobias had been so quiet, standing in the corner, his hands clasped behind his back through Hanna's many attempts to reach her friend, that Jake had nearly forgotten their host. He ran a self-conscious hand through his hair. "It's this postcard."

The nurse stepped forward. "When we moved her into this unit, she only brought a few personal items. That was one of them. I've always considered it one of her prized possessions."

"I think I know why." Jake handed the postcard to Hanna. Would she see the same thing he had?

Her eyes filled with questions, Hanna gave the image on the front of the card only the briefest of glances before she turned it over. "It's addressed to Dottie…" She paused, reading. "Wait. It's from me?"

"Go ahead, read it," Jake urged when tiny lines formed on Hanna's forehead.

"But…" She shrugged and took a breath. "Okay." She traced the words with one finger. "Darling Dottie," she read. "I'm finally in my new place in the big city. Address below. Can't write more because it's blazing hot." Her voice trailed off. When she raised her head, confusion and awe played tag across her face. "That's my handwriting and my signature. But that doesn't make any sense. I never lived in a city."

Jake pointed to the spot where she'd left off. "Keep reading," he urged.

"Okay." She held the card up to the light. "PS. We made it in time to celebrate our third year of bliss. Yours, Hanna." Her head tilted. "Dated, August sixteenth, 1946." Her voice faded to a soft murmur. "That's our anniversary."

Over her head, Jake traded a knowing look with Tobias. The old man had seen the card before. He might have even read it without having any idea of its significance. But now…

Wonder filled Hanna's voice. "Chet made it home."

Jake's heartbeat raced when an emotion he'd never seen her express banished all of Hanna's fears and concerns. The joy that replaced them was a thing to behold, and he swallowed. If he'd had any doubt about Hanna's love for Chet, her reaction had pushed those questions aside. Envy filled him. One day, he wanted to love someone as much as Hanna loved Chet.

She stared at the card as if it was a jigsaw puzzle

she'd assembled without ever seeing the picture. "They said he was lost in the war, but he—he made it home. That's why his name wasn't on the memorial. Chet didn't die."

"Hanna." Jake shoved his own longing aside to focus on hers. Quietly, he urged her to consider another significant part of the message. "If you wrote the card in 1946, that means Chet wasn't the only one who got to go home. It means you get home, too." He stood still, waiting for the truth to sink in.

"But…" Questions bloomed in Hanna's blue eyes. In a halting motion, she rocked back and forth on her heels. "But… how?"

That was the million dollar question, wasn't it? He turned to Tobias. The elderly gentleman stood, staring at Dottie as if he, too, had fallen into a trance. But unlike Dottie's, Tobias's disconnect only lasted a moment.

Waking, he snapped his fingers. "She didn't say *comment*," he said urgently. "She said *comet*." He tugged the card from Hanna's hands and flipped it over. His gnarled finger tapped the image. "It's a comet!" he announced. "C'mon, there's something at the house we need to see."

And with that, Tobias headed toward the door faster than most men in their eighties could muster, leaving Hanna and Jake no choice but to hustle after him.

Chapter Eleven

ack at the elegant home on Main Street, Hanna concentrated on taking slow and even breaths while the two men searched Toby's shelves for a book he insisted held the answers to everything. She wasn't sure that was possible. Too much had happened for it all to be explained in a few pages. It'd take more than a full set of encyclopedias to clarify how Chet had survived the war when all the reports said he hadn't. And that was just the first of many items on what had rapidly grown into a long list of mysteries she needed to solve.

"Chet is still alive," she said in a muted tone. She tried to wrap her mind around the idea. She squeezed her eyes tight. She'd been willing to stay in this time, to start a new life here, find a new purpose with these people. But knowing that Chet had made it home changed everything. Now, she had to get back, too. No matter what it took or what challenges she faced, she'd do anything—even catch a ride on a comet—if it meant getting back to her own time and her husband.

"Aha! Found it!" Brandishing a thin volume, Toby turned away from the shelves. "I knew it was in here somewhere." He hurried around the polished mahogany desk and sank into a plush leather chair.

Glad for the chance to take a break from her thoughts, she joined Toby and Jake. "Oh, the De Vico Comet," she said, reading the dust jacket before Jake took the book from Toby's outstretched hand. "That's the one everyone was talking about." She pointed to the man who looked so different, so much older, than the boy she'd known. "And you said that people were calling it the Christmas Comet, but that wasn't its real name." When Toby responded with a blank stare, she prodded. "Remember? It was just a few days ago."

"A few days for you," Toby said, giving her a knowing look. "Seventy years for me."

"Seventy-one, to be exact," Jake put in. After consulting the book's table of contents, he flipped through several sections until he found what he wanted. "Here we go." In a smooth voice, he read, "The De Vico is a periodic comet with an orbital period of seventy-one years. It was discovered by Francesco de Vico in 1874 on December 22th."

Toby stroked his beard. "Today."

Okay, this is all well and good, but how does it explain anything? More importantly, how can it help me get home? She swept a searching gaze over both men. "But what does that mean?"

"Ahhhh. Let me try and make some sense of this." Toby rose from his chair and paced the room. When he reached the fireplace, he turned toward them. "That last day in the hospital, I overheard the nurses talking." His gaze sharpened until it zeroed in on her. "Dottie was beside herself. They'd found your car in the snow. But you were gone, vanished." He snapped his fingers, the sound echoing through the otherwise quiet space. "Someone mentioned the coincidence of a comet the night before and—" An abashed grin drifted down over his face. "I was a boy, alone. I had a *wild* imagination. And I had a belief... in the magic of miracles."

"Yes." She remembered that day as if it was yesterday. "You wondered if rain was a miracle. If it was, you were sure the comet had to be one." She smiled. *Oh, to be eight again.*

"Well, Hanna. Think about it—a comet that only comes once every seven decades. At Christmas. On the night that you disappeared... and ended up here."

Toby's firm conviction stirred a fresh hope in her midsection. Struggling to accept the possibility that he was right, she pressed a hand below her waist. She felt herself teetering on the edge. She wanted to believe, willed herself to have faith. But her doubts crowded in. Why her? Wouldn't something like the chance to visit the future go to someone who deserved it?

She certainly wasn't that person. She wasn't a hero like Chet or the other boys who'd risked their lives in the war. She'd never done anything special. She hadn't changed the world for the better, or for the worse. The little flame of faith Toby had ignited in her heart guttered. "But why?" she asked out loud. "Why me?"

The words had scarcely left her mouth when Toby's two dogs bolted into the room. Tails wagging, the retrievers ran straight past their owner and made a beeline for her. Whining, they nosed her hands. While Toby commanded them to sit and behave, the would-be service dogs made a nuisance of themselves. Finally, she kneeled down and petted them both.

"Oh, good dogs," she cooed at the pair. She buried her fingers in their thick coats, surprised at how much calmer she felt when she'd run her hands through their fur. "Toby," she said when the dogs had had their fill of being petted, "those two might be too rambunctious for a lot of things, but they can definitely sense when someone is troubled. See how much they've helped me?"

"That's it." Jake clapped his hands together. "You wanted to know why you're here? Why all this happened to you? I think it's to show you, to show all of us..." With a sweeping gesture, he took in the room and the town beyond it.

What?

Whatever Jake meant to say, he needed to make it a whole lot clearer, because she hadn't received the message. In her frustration, she swung toward Toby. "To show us *what*?" she demanded.

As Ralph and Rex raced to his side, Toby pointed. "This! For the dogs. For this house. For you being here.

For me. For Jake. You've made such a difference in all our lives. Don't you see what you've done, Hanna?" He shook his head. "And the biggest miracle of all is that you didn't even know you were doing it."

Her lips parted while she soaked in Toby's words. No, she hadn't done much. She'd never been a hero in the strictest sense of the word. She'd never sacrificed her life on a battlefield or rushed into a burning building to save a child. But she had returned a dog to its owner on a snowy night. She'd expressed her concerns for a little boy who might have otherwise spent Christmas alone in an orphanage. She'd danced with a policeman. Those simple acts of kindness had had far-reaching effects. Because of Ruffin, people all over the country had the service dogs they needed. The town of Central Falls owed its library and science fair to a boy who'd been adopted because of events she'd set in motion. Thanks to the jealousy she'd sparked between them, Jake and Sarah were beginning to open their eyes to one another.

The thought was beyond humbling. Bowing her head, she gave thanks for all the lives she'd touched. "The smallest stone makes a ripple in the water." Her words broke the silence. She searched Jake's and Toby's faces. "That's what Dottie said. I was feeling so lost. Like I… I had no purpose."

"But you do," Toby insisted. "The rain. The comet. Christmas. They're all miracles." He gazed at her, his expression pensive. "Do you believe in miracles, Hanna?"

Warmth spread through her chest. It radiated out

to fingertips, her toes. Did she believe in miracles? "I think so," she answered, growing more certain by the second. In fact, she *knew* she did.

Toby leaned forward until the smallest gap separated their faces. "Then believe tonight that the Christmas Comet is going to come and take you back home."

His thinning voice broke something loose in her chest. The intensity of his gaze freed her of doubt. The strength of his words offered the assurance she needed. She swung a glance at Jake. The tall deputy nodded encouragingly. It wouldn't take much, he seemed to be saying. All she had to do was believe.

Okay, she could do this. She could believe that a miracle would take her home again. It wasn't that much of a stretch, not really. Not when she considered the ornaments and her camera, Toby and Dottie, the postcard. When she put all of those things together, she had enough evidence to prove that miracles did exist. What else would it take to convince herself that she was going home?

She closed her eyes and mouthed the words. *I believe. I believe.* A tingling sensation spread through her. Still, she refused to stop until her heart and her head accepted the truth. "I'm going home again," she said with an unwavering faith. "The Christmas Comet is coming to take me home."

Once everyone took a breath, Toby suggested they work out the particulars. "As you can imagine, I've read a lot about time travel." He gestured toward the shelves crowded with books that ranged from research on quantum physics to the latest in science fiction. "Though it's far from an exact science, there are a few things that remain the same throughout all the accounts. First, you'll need to return to the exact same place you were on the night of the comet."

"That part's easy." That, she remembered very clearly. "I was in the storage shed. I'd kneeled down because the thunder was so loud that the walls were shaking. I was afraid the roof would collapse." And the next thing she'd known, it was 2016.

"Good thing it didn't," Jake remarked.

"Yeah, that was pretty scary." She crossed her fingers and hoped the return trip wouldn't be so frightening.

"Okay, next, we'll need to recreate everything, down to the last detail. So, Hanna—" Toby's eyes skimmed over the modern clothes she'd borrowed from Louise. "You still have the dress you were wearing that night, don't you?"

"Oh, yes!" She'd hung it in her closet at the Stantons'. Briefly, she ran down the list of everything she'd had with her that night. Her shoes, coat and hat were all there, but… Concern etched its way across her brow. "I'm afraid I'll forget something."

"We'll help you remember." Encouragement filled Jake's nod. "You'll need your purse. I'll swing by the station and get it out of the evidence locker," he promised. "Your vial of Lune de Paris is in my desk. I'll get that, too."

"Okay. That takes care of her clothes and the

location. What else? What was going on in Central Falls that night?" Toby stroked his chin thoughtfully.

"Practically everyone in town had gathered for the lighting of the gazebo," she recalled. "I remember driving by on my way to take Ruffin home. People were singing carols and drinking hot chocolate. But… no one does that anymore." The thought was so sad that it made her heart hurt just to think of it.

"Oh, but you're wrong about that." A broad smile lit Jake's face. "That's another thing you've changed, Hanna. Everyone had such a good time caroling around town last night, I just bet they'll want to do it again tonight."

"And the lights!" Toby snapped his fingers. "You found the decorations for the gazebo earlier. Workers have been there all day, hanging the ornaments and putting up a Christmas tree. We can have an old-fashioned lighting ceremony tonight. We just need let everyone know about it."

"Leave that to Sarah and me," Jake offered. "We'll spread the word through the police department." He chuckled. "And Belinda Jones."

"Well, that's it, then. I need to get back to the farm and change my clothes." Hanna took a beat. It sounded as though they'd thought of everything. But she couldn't shake the idea that she'd forgotten something. "Is there anything else?"

"You have the key to the storage locker at the library, don't you?"

"Oh, darn. That was in my coat pocket, wasn't it?"

Thankful she hadn't left it at the library, she patted the pocket of the camel-colored coat Gretchen had loaned her. She let out a sigh of relief when her fingers traced the outline of the metal object. Her mind settled, she spun a last look around Toby's home. "I'll see you later at the town square?" she asked the man who'd given her hope.

But Toby only shook his head. "I wasn't there that night. I was still in the hospital," he said in answer to her knitted brows. "It might jinx things if I showed up at the gazebo tonight. It's better if we don't take that chance."

"So this is goodbye then? Will I never see you again?" At the thought, some of her joy ebbed away.

"Oh, I think you might. I still have your camera, remember?" Toby's face crinkled. A teasing light twinkled in his eyes. "When you get back, come and visit me in my new home, and I'll return it to you."

"That's right!" By the time she made it home to 1945, Sue Bunce would have already been to the hospital and made arrangements for young Toby to spend Christmas with his new family. She slung her arms around the man who'd made it possible for her to go home, too. "It's a date," she promised, hoping. "I'll see you again soon."

Ending the embrace, she swiftly crossed the room and bolted through the door before she teared up. Outside, cold air slapped her in the face and shook her confidence. As much as she looked forward to seeing young Toby, she had to admit, the whole idea of traveling back in time made her knees wobble. What if it didn't work? What if, instead of returning to 1945, she got lost in some other time, some other place? Did she really want to risk everything in the here-and-now on a slim possibility? No one could guarantee she'd ever get home again.

But if it works, isn't it worth the risk?

She took a breath and stopped to remind herself what she stood to gain by returning to the past. In exchange for her new friends, her new life, she'd regain her husband. She'd find love again. She'd have Chet.

She didn't have to ask what he'd do under similar circumstances. She already knew the answer to that question. When the call came, her husband hadn't wavered. He hadn't hesitated. He'd put his life on the line to protect his family, his home, his country.

Now that she faced the unknown, the uncertain, could she do any less?

"I'm going to miss you all so much," she said, aware that Jake had followed her from Toby's house. Turning, she faced the deputy. "I don't know what's going to happen. Will it work? Will I get back? I don't know, but I'm going to try," she promised. "Because… my life isn't this one. I don't belong here."

She belonged in 1945, with her husband and the life they were destined to live.

A potent mix of nerves and wonder swirled in Jake's chest as he waited for Hanna. He propped his hip against one cushion of the comfy recliner in the living room of his parents' home. Normally, the sights and sounds of the holiday season filled him with a sense of calm and happiness. But today, the candles burning in their holders failed to soothe him, the jolly Santa on the side table gave him no joy, the scent of mulled cider and evergreen jiggled his stomach. Unable to relax, he tapped a foot against the hardwood floor in an attempt to burn off some of his nervous energy. For the tenth time in as many minutes, he checked his watch.

What was taking so long?

Hanna had disappeared into her room to change clothes nearly an hour ago. It wouldn't be long now before the comet streaked across the sky above Central Falls. If she didn't come back soon, she'd miss the only window of opportunity she'd ever have to go home again.

"Patience, son," his dad counseled from his end of the couch. "If you haven't already figured it out, you should know that you're going to be waiting for a woman for the rest of your life. Trust me. It's worth it." His fingers moving in a circular motion, he stroked his wife's shoulder.

"I hear you, Dad." Under normal circumstances, he'd agree. But these were anything but normal circumstances, weren't they? A comet? Time travel? What if it didn't work? What if, despite all he'd done to help Hanna, she didn't make it back home? What if, instead, she froze to death in the storage shed while she waited for the miracle that wasn't going to arrive?

How would he have helped her then?

He scanned the faces of his family. His parents had taken the news of Hanna's impending departure better than he'd hoped they would. Rather than moping about after learning that her new friend was leaving, Gwennie had seized the concept of time travel and taken it to heart. His niece had pronounced the idea as *totally cool* and been jumping up and down with excitement ever since. If Louise had doubts, she'd kept them to herself, rather than burst her daughter's bubble. As for himself, he wished his own doubts weren't circling like vultures. He whispered beneath his breath, "I could use a boost of faith right now."

Snuggled next to his dad, his mom cocked her head and posed the very question that had been running through his mind. "So the Christmas Comet will get her home?"

In the pause that followed, he braced for his mother to pronounce the idea nuttier than her fruitcake. But she only sighed. With belief burning brightly in her eyes, she said, "There's something so *magical* about that."

"Seems a little *woo-woo* to me." From his corner of the couch, his dad rocked one hand in the air. The comment sent a tiny frown arcing across Gwennie's face and earned their father a pointed glare from Louise. The stern look must have hit its mark because in the next beat, he changed his tune. "But, hey, what do I know?"

Jake hid a silent laugh behind the palm of one hand when Gwennie only shrugged a tiny shoulder. His niece bounced up and down on the sofa. "Are *we* going to see the comet tonight?" She turned toward her mom. "Please, please, please, please," she begged.

"Okay, that's enough." Louise placed a restraining hand on her daughter's knee. The motion stopped the bouncing, at least temporarily, but it did nothing to dampen Gwennie's enthusiasm. His parents—and even Louise—chuckled when the little girl stared up at her mom.

"Puh-leeeeeeese," she begged.

It'd take a far, far stronger man than him to refuse those pleading eyes, Jake thought. He wasn't a bit surprised when Louise only held up her hands in surrender. "Yes," she said, giving in.

"Yay!" With an excited yelp, Gwennie hopped off her cushion.

"Shhh," Louise admonished, but her stern look didn't fool Jake, not for a second. Like his favorite chocolates, his sister had always hidden the softest of hearts beneath a firm outer shell. A shell that melted whenever Gwennie turned those big doe-eyes of hers on her. Not that he could fault Louise at all. In all likelihood, he'd be an absolute marshmallow when it came to disciplining his own kids, he admitted.

Of course, that implied he'd ever find the right

woman and settle down. Or that she'd have him. Neither of which was apt to happen any time soon.

He checked his watch for the umpteenth time and breathed a sigh of relief at the sound of footsteps in the hall. Across the room, Gwennie fell silent. His mom and dad straightened. Louise turned toward the doorway just as Hanna stepped into the living room.

He gave her outfit a practiced once-over. Hat, dress and coat. Check, check and check. On her feet, she wore the same red shoes that Louise had referred to as pumps. The only thing missing was her purse, so, standing, he placed the bag he'd removed from the evidence locker into her shaking fingers. "Nervous?" he asked half under his breath.

Hanna's pale face peered up at him from beneath her hat. "What if it doesn't work?"

Jake scanned the room for help. He knew better than to look for support from the man who didn't believe in time travel. Louise had already draped a sheltering arm around Gwennie's shoulders, as if to ward off doubt and fear. That left his mom. Only a few minutes ago, she'd been talking about magic. Surely, she'd weigh in on the subject now that they needed her support.

But doubt clouded the intensity of his mother's blue eyes, and Jake swallowed.

Now what?

In the beat that followed, Gwennie leapt from her place on the couch. Her little legs churning, she ran to

Hanna's side. "You said you believed in miracles," she said in a voice filled with fervor and insistence.

Hanna gave a sad smile. "I do, but—"

"And Mr. Cook said that you have to believe in something before it can *become* something."

"Of course you do. He's right," Hanna agreed. "Otherwise…"

Jake's thoughts raced. Gwennie was right. Throughout history, mankind had made great strides when people believed in the impossible. Would the world still be sitting in the dark if Thomas Edison hadn't believed enough in the concept of incandescent light bulbs *before* he'd invented them? If Niépce hadn't believed he could create pictures by treating paper with silver chloride, would Hanna have her camera? Space travel had been impossible, but because people had believed they could do it, men had walked on the moon.

"There is no otherwise." He grinned at his niece. The little girl had given his faith just the boost it needed. To Hanna, to all of them, he said, "It's going to work."

"'Cause it's a Christmas miracle!" Gwennie chimed in while rekindled hope sparkled in Hanna's eyes.

Jake tapped his watch. It was time. "You ready?"

He gave himself points for waiting patiently with nary a foot tap while Hanna's gaze traveled across the room to his parents. "Don't make me say goodbye," she said, on the verge of tears.

"All right." Gretchen dabbed at her eyes with a

tissue she pulled from her sleeve. Across from her, Louise did the same.

Like mother, like daughter, Jake thought. For a moment, he worried how Gwennie would handle Hanna's leaving, but he needn't have given it a second thought. His niece flung herself into Hanna's arms for a fierce hug. When they broke apart, Gwennie wore a grin that stretched from ear to ear.

"Time travel is exceedingly cool," she announced.

The quip was exactly what they needed to break the tension. In fact, he and Hanna were still laughing about it as they climbed into his car a few moments later.

Chapter Twelve

Without saying a word, Hanna moved from the seat of Jake's car to the sidewalk that cut through the center of the town square. At the end of the short path that led from the gazebo, the storage shed loomed larger than she remembered. Her grip on the handle of her purse tightened. So much had happened since she'd woken up, alone and shivering, on a stack of empty sandbags nearly a week ago. She'd gotten a glimpse of a future that was far more advanced than she'd ever dreamed possible. She'd lived in a world where people used tiny, pocket-sized devices to take pictures and talk to one another, where the inside of a car had more buttons and gadgets than the dashboard of an airplane, where the answer to any question she could think to ask was literally as close as her fingertips.

And yet, in spite of all the new technology, Central Falls and the people who lived there hadn't changed—

they were as kind and caring in 2016 as they'd been in 1945. When she'd shown up out of nowhere, they'd taken her in. Instead of throwing her in jail or in a psychiatric facility, they'd fed her, clothed her, and welcomed her into their homes. Jake and Sarah, Louise and Gwennie, Gretchen and Mark, Toby and, as much as she was able, Dottie—they'd all gone far, far out of their way to give her the help she'd needed.

As a result, she'd received the greatest gift she could imagine—she'd found her sense of purpose. No, no one would ever write a textbook about her. She'd never execute feats of daring. She wasn't going to cure cancer or invent a device that improved the lives of millions. But her life still had meaning. Her actions—as inconsequential as she'd thought they were at the time—had set much larger wheels in motion. Because of her, an orphaned boy had found a home, the disabled had service dogs, and the town of Central Falls had its own library.

And that was enough. It was all she'd really wanted, to know she'd done something with the life she'd lived. She could return to her own time now, content that no matter how small a stone she was, she'd make her own ripples in the world.

Her footsteps quickened as she and Jake approached the barn. She reached for the handle on the door, eager to move on to the next stage of her life, eager to return to Chet.

"Wait, Hanna."

At Jake's words, she glanced over her shoulder at

the handsome deputy who'd come to mean so much to her. A single glimpse of the stricken expression on his face stopped her in her tracks. Slowly, she turned to face him. A sense of loss settled in her chest. Without talking about it, she knew the same emotion tugged on his heart. "Don't say anything," she said, firming her resolve along with her smile. "I wasn't crying when I left, and we're supposed to keep everything the same, right?"

"You're right. It's just tough to say goodbye. That's all." He scuffed one boot through the snow. "I'll miss you."

Saying goodbye, whether to a friend or a loved one, was never easy. But Jake would be all right. He just needed a little reminder of the good things in his future. Lucky for him, she knew just how to go about it. "These last few days, you've become such a good friend," she began. "You stood by me when others were willing to write me off as some kind of lunatic. Or a, a con artist—that was the phrase Sarah used, wasn't it?" She waited, pleased to see a grin tug at the corner of Jake's lips.

"She didn't mean it." He shrugged and lifted his palms. "She just needed a little while to warm up to you."

"Sometimes, that's all we need. A little time." Aware that theirs had grown short, she plunged ahead. "I met my husband when I was six. He used to pull my pigtails. And I… I thought he was such a nuisance." As she had with Toby when he was just a boy, she made a face. And, just as it had with Toby, the action caused Jake to grin, too. Enjoying the moment, she waited a bit before she sobered. "Turns out, I was the last to realize that he was the love of my life. Just like you and Sarah are for each other."

"Sarah?" Denial swam in Jake's eyes. His mouth dropped open.

"Don't you try to pull the wool over my eyes, Jake Stanton." She fought down the nearly irresistible urge to prop her fists on her hips. "I've see the way you look at her. And I've seen how she looks at you, too. What was it when you were kids? Pigtail pulling? Or did you hide her books?"

Jake gave a guilty smile. "I used to put snow down her jacket. Of course, she did worse to me." His smile faded. "The difference is, I outgrew all that a long time ago. She's still a brat, though."

"And you wouldn't know what to do without her. You just haven't realized it yet. But you will. You two look at each other the same way Chet and I did."

Jake turned pensive while, somewhere close by, car doors slammed. Voices drifted across the snow. A man with a nice tenor launched into a Christmas carol. Within seconds, others joined him.

"It's time," Jake said. People were beginning to gather for the lighting of the gazebo… and the arrival of the comet.

"I know," she said softly. She needed to go inside and get ready well before the first golden streaks appeared in the night sky. She studied Jake's face. She had so much more she wanted to say, but their time had all but come to an end.

"Chet is a lucky man," Jake said.

"Sarah is a lucky woman." She was glad for whatever small part she'd played in bringing them together. Turning away from him before she lost her courage, she tugged the heavy door ajar. The icy cold of the handle penetrated her gloves, and she shivered.

"Hanna."

Her foot wavered over the threshold. At last, she shifted to look at him one more time.

"If this works and you get back," he asked, peering at her through eyes filled with hope, "do you think you'll remember all of this?" He swept one hand through the air.

It was a question worthy of an answer, and she wished she had one to give him. Instead, she shrugged. "I don't know," she said simply. "Who can predict a miracle?"

With that, she stepped into the barn and pulled the door shut behind her. She'd like to think she'd retain some of her memories of this time—the people she'd met, the friends she'd made, the things she'd seen. But not if doing so changed one single thing in her destiny or the future she and Chet would share together. Nothing was worth giving up that.

On the other side of the thick wood, she heard Jake slide the padlock into place, heard his hesitation. She took a breath and spoke through the door. "You have to lock it, Jake."

"Are you sure?" Muffled by the door, Jake's voice sounded very far away.

She spoke louder. "You heard Toby. We don't know what effect overlooking a single detail might have. The door was locked when I woke up that morning. I had to climb out the window. We can't change that. You have to lock me in here."

Several seconds passed before she heard a harsh metallic click that told her he'd done as she'd asked and sealed her inside.

"Thanks," she whispered as the sound of Jake's footsteps receded into the distance.

The die had been cast. The rest was up to a miracle.

Worrying her lower lip, she eyed the interior of the shed. When the comet had first appeared, she'd been cowering on the floor, afraid that the storm would bring the roof crashing down on her head. But when she'd woken, she'd been lying on the stack of empty sandbags in the corner.

Which position was the right one? Which one would get her home, and which would leave her stranded in a time that wasn't her own?

She mulled the question over for several long minutes before she pulled out the key she'd transferred to her coat pocket. A number had been stamped into the metal on one side, the name of the manufacturing company on the other.

"Heads, the floor. Tails, the sandbags." Whatever happened next, it was beyond her control. With a prayer, she tossed the key into the air and caught it in the palm of her hand.

Jake strode away from the shed, his footsteps confident and certain. He marched on until the sound of the snow crunching beneath his boots couldn't possibly penetrate the sturdy wooden walls of the old barn. He stopped then, leaned his shoulder against a nearby tree and took a minute.

Would the Christmas Comet really help Hanna make her journey back to Christmas in 1945? Or were they only setting themselves up for heartbreak?

Logic and rational thought insisted that he race back to the barn and unlock the door. Then, on the off-chance that Hanna had been fooling them all along and had simply decided that it was time for her to move on to another town, another place, she'd be free to leave.

But his heart—ah, his heart.

His heart argued for a miracle, a miracle that depended on everything being exactly the same as it had been the moment Hanna had woken up in 2016. That day, the door to the barn had been locked. As she'd insisted, it was now, too. Didn't he have to honor her wishes?

Satisfied that the choice had been hers, he gave the little shed one last glance over his shoulder before he hurried down the path toward the gazebo.

Reaching the edge of a small copse of trees, he slowed to a halt again. His eyes widened until the skin around them stretched tight as he stopped to stare at the scene in front of him. Not a creature had stirred on the town square when he and Hanna had traipsed through the park only a short while earlier. Now, so many people crowded the area that it looked as if the entire town had gathered for the lighting ceremony. Scanning the group, he spotted Chief Munson chatting with the mayor at the end of the sidewalk. George Jones stood nearby, and, judging by the calf eyes the boy aimed at a tall, brown-haired girl, the teen had traded his obsession with cell phones for a new love. All decked out in a red coat with a white scarf, Jessica Lipscomb moved through the crowd, carrying a large cardboard box. She stopped to talk with adults and share jokes with children as she handed out candles in red paper cups. At the edge of the gathering, Hal Jones took one from the box and tried to hand it to his wife, who only batted his efforts aside.

As she did practically everything else in Central Falls, Belinda watched her son's every movement like a hawk. When her attention never wavered and her perpetually pursed lips tugged even lower at the corners, sympathy for George stirred in Jake's chest. Deciding the young man and his sweetheart deserved a brief moment of privacy, he stepped between the town busybody and her current prey. While his wide shoulders blocked her view, he held out his palm to the boy. "Hand me your phone," he said to the teen. "I'll take a picture or two."

His heart warmed at the bright flare of intelligence that glinted in George's eyes. Not one to shy away from an opportunity, the boy took the chance to snuggle closer to his girlfriend.

Jake gave the pair a lopsided grin while he snapped a couple of shots. He issued a good-natured, "Behave yourselves," before he returned the phone. When George nodded a promise, Jake continued his trek through the group to his own family.

As he stepped to Louise's side, his mom turned questioning eyes toward him.

"Hey, Ma," he said, giving her shoulder a reassuring squeeze. Yes, he nodded, he'd done his best to help Hanna get home. They had to trust a miracle to do the rest.

Focused on the comet, Gwennie didn't appear to notice the drama unfolding around her. Her head tipped, his niece studied the sky where stars twinkled against the black velvet expanse. "When's it going to get here? My neck is gonna fall off!"

While Jake fought to keep from laughing out loud at the little girl's complaint, his sister swooped down over her child and hugged her daughter tight. "It's not for a while, silly," she said, her voice filled with love and warmth. "We're going to watch the gazebo lights go on."

"When will that be?" Gwennie rubbed her neck.

According to his mom, the mayor had announced

that he'd flip the switch about an hour before the comet's arrival. Jake checked his watch, but the answer to Gwennie's question died on his lips as movement on the other side of the park caught his eye.

Her hair loose and flowing about her shoulders, Sarah stepped out of the shadows into a pool of light. Around her neck, she wore the scarf he'd given her last Christmas, and Jake smiled. His smile deepened into a grin as he noticed that she'd traded her uniform in for a red jacket that cast a rosy glow on her face. His heart thudded almost painfully against his ribcage. The world spun around with Sarah at its center.

How had he overlooked the one person who'd been right in front of him all along? He'd known Sarah for most of his life. They'd laughed and joked, commiserated over disappointments, and celebrated successes together. In short, they'd been more than the best of friends—they'd been partners.

Is this love?

The answer seared through his chest, branding her name on his heart. His mouth went dry.

But does she feel the same way about me?

He thought back, searching for clues, and found what he was looking for in the familiar way Sarah had reached out to place a hand on his arm when they were alone or brushed her fingers across the sleeve of his jacket in the squad car. Her reaction when she'd spied him dancing with Hanna made sense… *if* Sarah was jealous… *if* she loved him.

He rubbed his head. Hanna had known the truth.

His mother, even his sister, had seen what he'd been blind to. Now that he saw it, too, he didn't want to waste another minute of the future he and Sarah might share together. Slipping away from the rest of his family, he edged through the crowd toward her.

He timed his footsteps to match hers as he stepped into Sarah's path. Last-minute doubts nibbled at his confidence. Did he really want to do this? Did he really want to profess his love for her and risk losing... everything? Because once he took this step, there was no going back. No returning to the way things had been between them. If her feelings for him weren't the same as his, he didn't think he could bear to be around her anymore. Couldn't work with her day in and day out, couldn't play the part of the goofy older brother whenever she visited his sister. No, if they weren't meant to be together, he'd have to move on, leave Central Falls and his family, and make a life for himself somewhere else, somewhere where Sarah wasn't.

His breath shuddered in his chest.

But if she did love him, if he and Sarah could share a love like the kind his parents had, he'd be content for the rest of his life. If their love grew until it transcended time, like Hanna and Chet's, he'd consider himself the luckiest man in the world. By the same token, if they had the chance for a love that poets would write sonnets about, but he let it slip away, he'd never forgive himself.

Wasn't it worth risking everything to find out?

It was, and for once—probably for the first time ever—he let his guard down completely. He inched closer until he closed the distance between them. He knew the moment Sarah realized that something had changed. His pulse raced at her slow double-take.

"What… ?" She tilted her head until her blue eyes gazed straight into his.

Do I really have to say it?

He couldn't trust his voice, not with so much resting on the next few minutes. Instead, he put his feelings into action.

Not wanting to hurry the moment, he took his time wrapping his arms around her. His chest expanded when she edged closer to him. Though it took every ounce of restraint he had in his being, he resisted the urge to seal his wordless pledge to her with a kiss that would leave no room for doubt. All too aware of where they were and how many of their friends, neighbors, and relatives crowded around them, he lowered his head and placed a single, lingering kiss on her forehead.

"Have you… lost it?"

He studied the hope that danced in her eyes despite her question. In the past, this had been the point where one of them made a joke, covered over their true feelings with a thick layer of banter while they each retreated into their comfort zone. But no more. The time had come to take a stand.

"No," he said. "Actually, I think I found it."

The world stood still while he waited for her

reaction. Would she tap him playfully on the shoulder and pretend that what they shared didn't really exist? Or would she drop all pretense and admit that they were made for each other and always had been?

The sights and sounds around them faded until only he and Sarah were left. His mouth, which had been dry before, turned into a desert. His temples pulsed. His breath stalled.

Just when he thought he'd pass out if she kept him waiting for her reaction a moment longer, a joyful smile graced the lips he wanted to spend the rest of his life studying. And without a word—not that words were necessary—Sarah snuggled into his arms. He pulled her close, pressing her to him until all he felt was her warmth, all he smelled was the flowery scent of her shampoo, all he touched was the nubby fabric of her coat. He held her until her pulse beat in sync with his own.

His heart swelled. She was his, and he was hers. Vowing that he'd never let her go, he pressed another kiss into her hair and wished the moment would last forever.

Long before he wanted to admit it had, cold seeped through the soles of his boots. Late arrivals jostled his elbows as they passed by. Snippets of conversations drifted to him on the night air. Awareness of the crowd around them sank in, and they pulled apart. Gazing into each other's eyes, they traded looks that promised… more… later. Letting go entirely was out of the question though, so he draped one arm around

Sarah's shoulders. Together, they headed for the spot where his family waited.

He braced for a barrage of questions from his mom and Louise, but thanked his lucky stars that the mayor chose that moment to climb the steps of the gazebo.

"Okay, everybody." The mayor's voice rang out. "Here we go. Ten… nine…"

Before he got any farther, the entire crowd joined in the countdown.

"Eight… seven… six…"

Gwennie clapped her mittened hands together. Around them, people aimed cell phones and cameras.

"Three… two… one."

Surprised gasps rose from the crowd as a bright holiday glow filled the park. The excitement grew until people were unable to contain it. At first, a smattering of applause tittered across the town square. In seconds, others had joined in until the whole town clapped and cheered.

Jake stood with his arms wrapped around Sarah while he gazed in wonder at the brilliant star that shone from the highest point of the gazebo's roof. From there, rows of twinkling lights fanned out to the eaves where glinting icicles dripped from every corner. Swags of brightly lit garland dipped and rose from posts anchored with red velvet bows. Under the pitched roof, the ornaments they'd taken from Hanna's storage locker reflected the lights on a Christmas tree that, as hard as it was to believe, outshone even his mom and dad's.

Somewhere in the crowd, a woman—though he told himself not to be ridiculous, Jake suspected Belinda Jones—launched into "The Twelve Days of Christmas." Before she reached the second line, a dozen voices had joined in the singing. People raised their candles as warmth and goodwill spread throughout the group. The cares of the season faded from the faces of the fathers. Mothers hugged their children tighter. Siblings set aside their rivalries. As for the lovers, he noticed that not even Mr. and Mrs. Jones were immune to the Christmas magic. And, smiling, he snuggled Sarah closer to his side.

Before the last partridge sat in a pear tree, the high school music teacher mounted the gazebo's steps. The moment the first song ended, he launched into another familiar tune, and the caroling continued. They were halfway through "Silent Night" when a shout rose from somewhere behind Jake.

"Look!"

The song sputtered. All around him, people stared into the night sky where a faint light glimmered. A collective gasp rose from the crowd. The light grew into an enormous glowing orb as it sped toward them. It streaked across the heavens, trailing a glittering fog.

Jake stood in open-mouthed wonder at the sight. Though he knew such things weren't even remotely possible, he swore he felt a magic dust rain down on him. "Safe journeys, Hanna," he wished.

Sarah tilted her face toward his. "What was that?"

"The magic of the night. It makes you feel like anything's possible."

"That it does." She stared up at him, her blue eyes filled with love.

He squeezed her tightly. His throat worked. "Want to go out with me sometime?" he asked. In his mind, he pictured candlelight and roses, fine china and linen napkins, violins playing softly in the background. He heard her quick intake of breath, watched her eyes widen as the reality that tonight was just the start of something magical struck home.

"People will think we're crazy," she said with that shy smile that told him she'd already made her decision.

"Let 'em. Let 'em 1701 us if they want to. In a way, they'll be right, 'cause I'm crazy about you in all the good ways."

She rose on tiptoe. "In that case, I accept." With the brush of her lips against his chin, she sealed the deal.

Unable to resist, he picked her up and swung her around, marveling that she felt as light as a feather in his arms.

Aware that they were being watched, he brushed a tender kiss onto her forehead and settled her back on the ground. Arm in arm, they turned to face the crowd who, for the third time that night, had found something to cheer about.

Chapter Thirteen

Reluctant to leave his pleasant dream behind, Jake rose out of a deep sleep in slow stages. Light filtered through his eyelids. He opened them and blinked. Where was he? Gradually, his confusion faded as he took in the checkered drapes that hung in his parents' living room, traced the outline of the pattern in their couch with his fingers, felt the stiffness that came from sleeping sitting up all night. An unfamiliar weight pressed against him, and he glanced down. Curled into him, Sarah slept soundly with her head on his chest. His heart stilled.

So, it hadn't been a dream after all.

Sarah cared for him as much as he cared for her. The fact that she was still here, that her hair spread a golden halo across his arm, that her soft breaths sighed against his cheek, proved it beyond a shadow of a doubt. He grinned as memories of the night before drifted into focus.

After the comet's final sparkle had faded from the night sky and the crowd had dispersed, the entire Stanton clan had gathered around the roomy island in the kitchen, where the family had toasted the start of a new relationship with mugs of hot chocolate and Christmas cookies. While Gwennie bounced up and down, unable to contain her excitement, he and Sarah had been treated to a year's worth of hugs, as well as a couple of I-told-you-so's. The latter primarily came from Louise and his mom, but even his dad had gotten in on the act when he'd issued a solemn "It's about time!" as they'd shaken hands.

"First dates are important," Louise had declared. "They set the tone for the entire relationship. So…" She pinned him with the insistent look only his sister could get away with. "Where are you taking my best friend?"

"Nothing like a little pressure," Jake had answered with the light confidence of a man who had the perfect evening all planned out. "Saturday night, we'll go into the city for dinner and a show."

"We can't go out on Christmas Eve," Sarah had protested. Her amused gasp had shattered his plans into a thousand pieces. "That's the night we hang up our stockings and read *'Twas The Night Before Christmas.* This year, Gwennie and I are going to track Santa's progress on the computer."

"I get to pick out the best cookies and carrots for him and his reindeer," his niece had boasted.

Jake had expelled a long, slow breath. Sarah was

right. There was something fitting and wonderful about spending the holidays surrounded by family. Silently, he'd thanked her for the reminder while he'd taken another, closer look at his plans. They couldn't drive into the city the following week. Chief Munson would have their heads if he and Sarah both asked to take off on New Year's Eve. Everyone on the force spent the long night of parties helping the good citizens of Central Falls stay safe.

"What's wrong with grabbing a pizza and taking a walk through the town square?" Sarah had asked.

"I suppose, since we've waited this long, we can hold off on the fancy stuff until we have something more to celebrate." Though he'd grumbled a bit about the change of plans, his heart hadn't been in it. Their first date—no matter what they did—would be perfect as long as they were together. He'd leaned down then and kissed the tip of Sarah's nose.

Later, after the last cookie crumb had been swept away, the mugs washed, and Gwennie tucked in for the night, he and Sarah had settled in on the couch in the living room. There, they'd talked and laughed for hours. He wasn't quite sure when they'd fallen asleep. Now though, the first rays of a new day filtered through the living room windows. A layer of fresh powder coated the fields and bushes.

Snow?

Snow hadn't been in the forecast when he'd checked the weather yesterday, but, according to Hanna, the last time the Christmas Comet had appeared in the sky over Central Falls, there'd been quite the snowstorm. And, unless he was mistaken, another one had blown through while they'd slept. He rubbed his eyes and took another look. Beyond the window, a white blanket coated the fields. It piled in drifts along the fences.

Beside him, Sarah slipped her hand under her cheek. Lying with her head on his chest, she looked so peaceful and serene that he struggled with the urge to stay right where he was. His heart lurched. Leaving her side was the last thing he wanted to do, but he'd agreed to meet Tobias at the barn first thing this morning.

Jake closed his eyes. What would they find there? Would Hanna be waiting for them on the other side of the door? Or had the magic of the Christmas Comet taken her home? He crossed his fingers and hoped she'd gotten her Christmas miracle, just like he'd gotten his. With a last, tender look at Sarah, he eased himself off the couch.

In the kitchen, he started the first pot of coffee for the day. Before the last few drops dribbled into the carafe, floorboards squeaked over his head. Aware that the house was stirring, he poured coffee for himself and doctored a cup for Sarah who, with a yawn, wandered in from the living room.

"I was bringing this to you." He lifted a mug and a smile in her direction.

"I missed you too much to wait for it," she said, her voice light and teasing.

That sounded an awful lot like an invitation to

steal a kiss. He settled the mugs on the counter. While the pitter-patter of little feet warned that the rest of the family would join them soon, he wrapped his arms around the girl who'd stolen his heart and pulled her close. They just had time for a quick embrace before a door closed upstairs and footsteps sounded on the stairs.

"What's the plan?" Sarah wanted to know, her head pressed against his shoulder.

"I told Tobias I'd meet him at the barn around seven." He planted another kiss on the crown of her head.

Sarah peered out the window. "It looks like we got a foot or more of fresh snow, and I don't think the roads have been plowed yet." She gave her chin a thoughtful tap. "Can we make it into town?"

Confident that his truck could handle anything short of a blizzard, Jake sipped his coffee. "Actually, the snow might work in our favor. It'll keep people indoors. Until we see what we're dealing with inside the barn, the fewer people there, the better."

"Well, just as long as you don't try to keep us away." His mom sailed into the kitchen.

"We're coming with you. If for no other reason than to offer moral support," his dad insisted, trailing his wife. He headed for the coffeepot, where he filled two mugs and handed one to Gretchen.

Footsteps pounded in the hallway. Seconds later, Gwennie burst into the kitchen dressed in jeans and a warm white sweater, her curls tamed, and the cheeks of her freshly scrubbed face glowing.

Jake tousled her hair. He gave Gwennie's mismatched socks a passing glance and caught the wistful stare Sarah had focused on his niece. Was there a cousin or two in Gwennie's future? Though it was far too early to be thinking along those lines, the thought ignited a warm glow in his midsection. A son to play catch with? A daughter who'd wrap him around her little finger even more tightly than Sarah had? He smiled. He could only hope.

"Mom!" Gwennie called when Louise appeared in the doorway a moment later. "I want to go with everyone to the barn." She tugged on her mom's hand.

"Don't worry, my love," Louise cooed. "We'll all pile in with Gram and Pop."

"Except for Sarah and me—we'll take my truck." He might not be able to prevent his family from coming along but, whatever the outcome, he and Sarah would see it through to the end, together.

A half hour and a few swerves on the icy roads later, truck doors slammed as they all piled out of their vehicles just beyond the town square. While they waited for Tobias to arrive, Jake circled the building. Not exactly sure what he expected—or wanted—to find, he tromped around the first corner. Undisturbed snow lay as far as he could see. He moved to the next corner and held his breath. He needn't have bothered. The smooth, white crystals continued in an unbroken layer around all four corners of the little shed. Unless she'd sprouted wings and flown away, Hanna hadn't left the building through either the door or the window.

By the time he finished the circuit, other townsfolk had shown up to add their support. Jake scanned the growing group. He spotted Sarah talking with the owner of the Organic Planet and moved to join them. That plan derailed when an inquisitive Dr. Lipscomb stepped in front of him. He traded greetings with the doctor, and, while he didn't think they'd spoken for very long, by the time they finished, Belinda and Hal Jones had traipsed from the parking lot, along with their son, George, and his new friend.

"What's going on, Deputy Stanton?" Belinda's voice broke the quiet of the morning as she struggled through a small snowdrift.

Tension tightened the muscles in his neck. Feeling as though he could use a small dose of moral support, Jake took Sarah's hand and cleared his throat. To put everyone's concerns at ease, he explained, "We all know Hanna Morse. We all know she didn't really fit in here. Well, last night, the Christmas Comet gave Hanna her one chance to go back to her own time, her own friends, her husband."

He swept a steady gaze over the small assembly. An agreeable murmur rose from those who'd gathered. All but from Mrs. Jones, that was. The town busybody pursed her lips and seemed on the verge of voicing an objection.

Before she had the chance, Gwennie covered her eyes. "I'm scared, Mommy!"

"Don't be, my love." Like a mother hen, Louise folded her little girl into her protective arms.

Jake drew in a deep breath of the icy air. Waiting around on pins and needles was hard enough on the adults. How much worse was it for the children? Though Tobias hadn't arrived yet, the time had come to take some kind of action. Leaving Sarah's side, he approached the barn.

"Hanna?" he called. When no one answered, he gave the heavy wood a hard rap. "Hanna?"

A restless murmur rose from the crowd behind him. He turned, intending to ask for silence. But just as he did, a long black sedan raced into view. Snow spraying from its tires, the car slid to a stop at the curb at the edge of the square. The engine still ticked and hissed when young Julius leaped from behind the wheel. Carrying a large manila envelope, he hurried to open the back door for his boss.

"He's here!" Gwennie called the moment Tobias stepped from the vehicle.

With Julius at his side, the older man hurried to join them. "Anything?" Tobias asked as soon as he got close enough to be heard.

Jake gave his head a slow shake. "I called out to her. There wasn't any answer."

"Well, we'll see then, won't we?" Tobias fished a key from his coat pocket, inserted it into the padlock and gave a firm twist. The instant the shackle fell open, the shed's owner removed the lock from the door and slipped it into his pocket.

This was it. This was the moment they'd all been waiting for.

Signaling everyone else to stand back, Jake pushed the door wide. He swore his heart stopped as he and Tobias stepped into the darkened barn. Inside, Jake's breath rose in a misty cloud while he scanned the four walls. A single beam of light came through the window so, pulling his phone from his pocket, he clicked on the flashlight app. He aimed the bright circle around the small room. It illuminated the pile of sandbags, the tools on the wall, the table… and nothing else. A shiver ran through him, but he couldn't tell whether the lingering sense of magic or the cold caused it.

"She's gone home." Tobias's awed whisper bounced off the walls of the small room. The small *empty* room. The old man expelled a heavy breath. "We have to tell the others." For a man of his age, Tobias moved fast. He spun toward the open doorway and hurried through it. As he stepped into the snow, sunlight glinted off the arm he raised in a victory sign. "She's home!"

Jake watched as the people around him absorbed the truth about what had happened. Wonder transformed his mother's face. Dr. Lipscomb gave her head an awed shake. The Jones boy pumped his fist in the air.

"We'll see about that," Belinda Jones huffed. She brushed past him and stepped into the barn. When she reemerged a few seconds later, her face bore a startled, confused expression. "She's gone," she stated in an odd voice. "She's really gone."

Wanting, *needing,* to share the moment with Sarah,

Jake grabbed her hand and gave it a squeeze. Bending low over her, he grinned. "She did it."

"I know." Sarah's head bobbed.

He traced one glove over her face. "Gwennie was right about that Christmas miracle all along." Wondering what the next visit of the De Vico Comet would bring, he slipped one arm around Sarah's waist and hoped they'd see it together.

Tobias cleared his throat. "Before you go," he called, "there's one more thing I'd like you to see."

At that, Julius placed a thick packet into the older man's waiting hand.

While anticipation built, Tobias waved the envelope through the air. "These are photos from Hanna's camera," he explained. Prying open the flap, he pulled out several glossy photographs which Julius dealt like cards into waiting hands.

Gwennie took one and tugged on Louise's sleeve. "Mommy, look at the little boy."

Smiling, Tobias squatted down beside her. He tapped the photo. "That's me."

A sense of déjà vu swept over Jake when he peered down at the photo of a youngster in the children's ward of a hospital. The boy in the metal-framed bed sported a heavy plaster cast, just like the one Hanna had described.

"Hey! Look at this one!" George turned the photo he held around so everyone could see. "That's the star we put on top of the gazebo."

The feeling that he'd been there, done that, grew

as Jake stared at the photo of a much-younger Dottie holding the star up to her face like a picture frame.

Someone handed Jake another photo. He took a quick look, intending to pass the picture along to the next person in the crowd, but his heart stuttered the instant he glanced down at the shiny black-and-white print. Faces he recognized from the family photo album his mom kept on the coffee table stared up at him. The hairs on the back of his neck stood up and saluted.

"Um, Mom?" he called, unable to keep his astonishment in check. "Look. That's Grams and Pops." He shoved the photo of the wounded soldier and the pretty nurse into his mother's hands.

"What?" A mix of wonder and delight filled his mother's face. She traced shaky fingers over the picture. Recognition dawned in her eyes. "Oh, it is!"

Jake studied the photograph. "Pops' leg is in traction. I bet this was taken right after he came back to the States." His grandfather had been awarded a Purple Heart for wounds he'd sustained during World War II. Proud of his contribution to the war effort, he'd walked with a limp to the day he'd died.

Slowly, his mom shook her head. "I knew they met in a hospital. Mom was a nurse. And it was just after the war." She lifted questioning eyes to Tobias. "Why would Hanna have a picture of my parents?"

A tender smile deepened the wrinkles on Tobias's face. "Hanna introduced them. She thought that would be a nice thing to do." He laughed. "It was.

If I remember right, Hanna took this picture the day Frank popped the question."

His mom continued to stare at the photo for a long moment. "If she hadn't done that one little thing, then…" Looking up from the picture, she swept a tearful gaze over the entire family.

Jake shivered. "Then none of us would be here," he finished, thinking about the miracle of big ripples caused by small stones.

"Come here, Gwennie," his mom called. As Jake watched, she snugged the little girl close to her. Though her hands still trembled, Gretchen held the picture out. "Look, honey," she said. "That's your great-grandmother and your great-grandfather."

Gwennie's eyes widened. "That's exceedingly cool," she pronounced.

Beside her, Tobias chortled. "Yes, it is," he agreed. "It sure is."

Jake stared into Sarah's blue eyes. He had far more to thank Hanna for than he'd ever realized, and, all too aware of the miraculous series of events that had put them together, he hugged the woman of his dreams closer to him.

Chapter Fourteen

A chill shivered down Hanna's back. She stirred awake. Her arms and legs felt stiff and cold. Her neck hurt. And no wonder. She had no pillow, no blankets. She pushed away from the rough wooden surface she must have been leaning against when she fell asleep. She sat straighter, anxious for the prickly sensation of pins-and-needles to subside so she could stand. When it did, she slid from what looked like a stack of empty sandbags and tightened her coat around her.

"Where am I?"

The bare walls didn't answer, but that was okay. It was all coming back to her. The lost dog, the blinding snow, her car sliding on the ice into a snow drift. Desperate to find someplace warm, someplace safe, she'd abandoned the vehicle and trudged through the cold and the wet to reach the barn near the gazebo.

Absently, she straightened her hat. She supposed

she ought to call for help next. She scanned the walls, hoping for a phone, though she told herself the chances the owner had installed one in the barn were all but nonexistent. Reaching for her purse, she found it dangling from her arm, exactly where it had been when she'd drifted off during last night's storm. She should have asked Jake to lend her a cell phone.

Wait. What was a cell phone? And who was Jake?

Slowly, she took a steadying breath. The icy cold that shimmied through her chest brought her all the way awake.

A dream, she decided as hazy images of sleek cars, and puffy coats, and electric beaters faded. She'd dreamed of the future. But she'd never met a tall, dark-haired Deputy Stanton. Not really. She'd never stayed in the Morgans' guest room. Never baked Christmas cookies with a girl named Gwen. Why, she hadn't even seen a comet, thanks to the blizzard that had struck Central Falls last night.

She shook her head, and the dream receded. No matter how vivid her visit to the future had been, none of it was real. "That'll teach me to fall asleep in a cold barn." Hoping it would help her shake off the last remnants of the strange dream, she said the words aloud. Her voice bounced off the walls. Her breath plumed in the frigid air.

A sense of urgency, of purpose, filled her, and she straightened. She had places to go, better things to do than to freeze to death in a storage shed.

A sturdy-looking table stood under the only

window in the room. She took a step toward it and stopped. Another gulp of air helped clear the last remaining cobwebs from her brain. Changing course, she headed for the door.

Snow spilled onto the floor as she pulled it open. Sunlight glinted off the clean, white blanket that lay over the sidewalks and piled in high drifts against the gazebo. A clear blue filled the skies overhead. An odd sensation stirred in her chest. She paused to examine it. Warmth flooded through her at the realization that, for the first time since she'd lost Chet, she felt happy. Happy knowing she'd returned Ruffin to his owners last night. Happy to have a job that let her make a difference in people's lives. Happy to simply be alive. She straightened her coat, fluffed her hair, and smiled. It was time she quit lying about and feeling sorry for herself. Time she rejoined the living.

She threw her shoulders back and stepped into the sunshine. Her foot sank through several inches of fresh snow. The cold crystals melted on contact. Water seeped into her shoes. She shrugged, took another step, and then another. She'd buy another pair of shoes if she had to. Hose, too, though those were dearer than hen's teeth. But no one was going to dig her car out of the snowbank for her. She'd have to do that herself if she expected to get to the hospital in time for her shift this afternoon.

Standing by the Hudson a short while later, she tsked. Her attempts to rock the car out of the snow had failed. The tires spun and slipped on the ice. That left digging the vehicle out by hand as her only choice, so, leaving her purse on the front seat, she scoured the area for some sort of tool. A downed tree limb lay nearby. She broke off a sturdy stick and went to work. A remnant of her dream floated back while she struggled to free the back tire.

Wouldn't it be nice to be able to press a few buttons and know that help was on its way?

But it made no sense to wish for the impossible so she dug another hole with the stick. After brushing away the snow she'd loosened, she eyed her progress. At the rate she was going, she wouldn't free the vehicle before spring. But standing around, waiting for the car to dig itself out wasn't going to work either.

Determined, she got a better grip on her stick and went back to work. She pried up a small clump of packed snow and flipped it aside. Surprised, she stepped back when a huge chunk of ice slid along with it. The move had freed the whole tire.

"Well, look at that," she gasped, nearly out of breath. "Dottie was right. One small stone can make a big ripple."

While someone whistled a jaunty tune in the distance, she put an extra dose of strength behind her next move. She could do this. It was hard work. It was sheer drudgery. She huffed and puffed like a steam engine. She'd probably ruined her new shoes. The wet snow had drenched the hem of her coat, and her hands hurt.

But she'd do it.

From somewhere nearby, a man's voice drifted through the early morning quiet. "Why not just get your husband to help you?"

Hanna stilled.

It couldn't be.

But she knew that voice. Its teasing lilt was as familiar as the back of her hand. Her heart in her throat, she glanced up from the particularly stubborn section of ice she'd been trying to free... and froze at the sight of a tall man wearing olive drab.

Chet?

She blinked. The man didn't move. He stopped whistling. The last notes of "I'll Be Home For Christmas" faded. She rubbed her eyes, afraid that, like her odd dream, he, too, would fade into nothingness. But no. No matter how hard she pressed her fingers to her eyelids, the man was still there when she opened them.

But it couldn't be Chet... could it?

Unable to breathe, she scrutinized the soldier. She'd recognize the grin she'd studied from grade school through graduation anywhere. The button on his uniform jacket sat ever-so-slightly askew. Hadn't she sewn it that way? From his polished shoes to the crisp pleats in his uniform pants, to the duffel bag he tossed onto a nearby snowdrift when he threw his arms wide, there was no doubt about it. He was her Chet.

How? Why? She refused to think about it. What does it matter?

And, letting the stick fall from her fingers, she flung

herself into his arms. It didn't matter how he'd gotten here. She didn't care why he'd shown up now instead of six months ago. None of that mattered. Nothing mattered except the warmth of his arms about her, the blend of woods and musk that was uniquely his, the familiar way her head fit into the notch just below his collarbones. She sighed as happy tears streamed down her cheeks. No matter how Chet had survived, no matter what stars had aligned, he'd come home to her.

He was her Christmas miracle... and she'd never let him go again.

Epilogue

"Do you want chocolate on your ice cream?" Sarah's voice floated through the screen door and onto the back porch of the cottage.

Jake thought for a half second. Normally, he liked nothing better than a good-sized squirt of syrup over a dish of vanilla. But Sarah's recent bout with a stomach virus had left her with an aversion to all things chocolate. If she'd sworn off them for the time being, he would, too. After all, he'd promised her for better or for worse. "And ruin that good taste? No, thanks."

"You're sure? I don't mind." The freezer door thunked closed.

"Nah. I'm sure." From his spot on the back steps, he stared out over his father's cornfield. The stalks stood tall, their golden ears ripening in the warm summer temperatures. Beyond the porch, the ground gently sloped upward to a fence, and beyond that to the house where he'd grown up, where his parents, Louise and Gwennie still lived. The first fireflies of the evening darted about, their green lights flickering against the last red rays of the setting sun. The colors reminded him of Christmas. Which was appropriate, he guessed, considering that the news he'd received today brought back a host of Christmas memories.

Gently, he smoothed his fingers over the photograph he'd taken from his back pocket at least once a day for the last six months. Thanks to constant handling, the image had frayed around the edges. A white line ran down its center, the crease no doubt created by the fold in his wallet. Despite the wrinkles, though, the picture Louise had snapped of Central Falls's only time traveler remained intact. Standing in the living room entryway, Hanna had managed a tremulous smile while she'd modeled clothes she'd borrowed from his sister. At the time, no one had known quite what to make of their guest. Certainly, no one had realized how much courage it had taken for her to function in a world that must have been altogether confusing and foreign.

Behind him, spoons rattled into dishes. Sarah's bare feet slapped the wooden floor he'd sanded and refinished just before the wedding. Anchoring one corner of the picture in a narrow crack in one of the planks, he hustled to his feet to get the door for her when her footsteps neared.

"I love it out here in the evening," she said, handing him one of the two bowls. "I was always glad when Louise asked me to sleep over in the summer. We'd pitch a tent right out there." She pointed to a spot under a leafy red maple as she lowered herself onto the step. "She and I would stay up half the night talking about boys and watching for shooting stars."

"And here I thought I was the only reason you and Louise were friends," he teased when they sat side by side.

"You wish." Sarah nudged him with her shoulder.

"You mean there were other boys?" He let a playful grin slip onto his face. "Besides me?"

"Hmm. Louise had her eyes on a new fella every week, but there was only one guy who held my interest. Now, hush and eat your dessert before it melts." Sarah scooped up a bite of hers.

For a few minutes, he savored the cool, creamy taste of ice cream made with milk from cows in their own barn, eggs from chickens they raised right here on the farm. This afternoon, he'd shown Gwennie how to layer ice and salt into the old-fashioned churn. Then, they'd taken turns spinning the crank until the concoction froze solid. As far as he was concerned, nothing tasted better in the world.

Well, nothing except Sarah's kisses. Those are beyond special.

"Maybe we should get chairs for out here. You can't be comfortable sitting on the steps," he suggested after he'd worked his way through half his ice cream. He'd buy them if she wanted—he'd do anything she asked—but there was a lot to be said about sitting right where they were. He especially liked the part that came next, when finished with dessert, he'd slide his arm around Sarah's shoulders and hold her close. They'd sit, talking about the day, what they had on tap for tomorrow. Together, they'd watch the fireflies until the last rays of daylight faded from the sky and it was time for bed.

"Maybe. One day. For now, this is fine." She tapped the bottom step with one toe. "You did a nice job with these."

A warm spot in his chest expanded. It meant a lot that Sarah liked the house he'd been working to restore ever since he'd finished college and come back home to live. The cottage had sat vacant after Grams and Pops had moved to the bigger place on the top of the hill. When he'd moved in, the small house had needed a complete makeover. He'd added the back porch before Christmas, installed all new appliances in the kitchen over the winter. Only the spare bedroom still needed work. He'd planned to get started on it last week, but had put it off while Sarah was under the weather. Now that she felt better, he supposed he'd get to it soon enough.

The edges of the photograph fluttered in the warm summer breeze that rippled across the field. Juggling his spoon and bowl in one hand, he retrieved the picture. He'd intended to return it to his wallet, but beside him Sarah stilled.

"You're still thinking of her?"

He couldn't see her face in the deepening shadows, but she sounded oddly unsure of herself. Hating the idea that she could even think of him and another woman, he set his half-finished bowl aside. The move freed his arm. He sidled close enough to cup her shoulder beneath his fingers.

"I think about Hanna a lot," he admitted. "I'll always be grateful that she came into our lives." Wanting to get the words right, he paused. They'd known Hanna for less than a week, but her presence in their lives had changed everything. Sarah needed to know why, six months later, he still held on to the memory of their visitor. He swallowed. "If it hadn't been for her, we'd probably still be dancing around our feelings for one another."

"Dancing," Sarah said wistfully. "Strange that you should use that particular word. Seeing her in your arms that day in your parents' living room stirred feelings I wasn't proud of."

So, he'd been right—she had been jealous of Hanna. But there hadn't been any reason for it then, just as there wasn't any reason for those feelings now. Hoping she could see the honesty reflected on his face, he turned toward her. "I'm a one-woman man, and you're it. I love you, Sarah Stanton. I always have. I always will."

He grasped her hand and traced over the simple gold band he'd slid onto her finger in front of all their family and friends on the first day of spring. Sarah had insisted on a simple ceremony in the town square. Gwennie, of course, had been their flower girl and Louise, the maid of honor. He'd asked his dad to be his best man, and his mom had taken charge of the decorations. When she'd promised to keep the fuss down to a minimum, Jake had smothered a smile. Sure enough, the gazebo had undergone a complete transformation in the weeks leading up to the wedding, a day he'd never forget.

Sarah leaned forward to press her nose against his. "I love you, too." She sighed and straightened. "But we've had the occasional odd duck wandering around Central Falls in the past. Remember that panhandler who came through here last year? You didn't go to bat for him like you did for Hanna." As if to emphasize the point, she tapped her spoon against the side of her bowl.

Jake nodded. He remembered. "That guy lied. He said he was a wounded warrior. A quick check of his fingerprints proved he hadn't even served in the military." By setting up shop on the corner of Main and Central, the pretender had earned himself a one-way ticket on the next bus out of town.

"I guess I've always wondered how you knew, right from the very beginning, that there was something different, something special about her."

He listened for the slightest hint that Sarah saw Hanna through green-tinted glasses. His shoulders relaxed when he heard only curiosity in her tone. The knot in his chest untied itself. He could handle her questions. In fact, he wanted to answer all of them. "I didn't actually," he confessed. "Chalk it up to the season. Now, I'm not going to lie to you—break the law in Central Falls and you'll get arrested, no matter what the season. But Hanna hadn't committed any 'crime.'" Borrowing the gesture from Sarah, he traced finger quotes through the air. "She just didn't know where—*or when*—she was. It didn't seem fair to treat her like a criminal. Giving her a place to regain her bearings was the right thing to do."

"You did more than that, and it didn't stop there," Sarah pointed out. "What you did—helping her get back home—it affected all our lives."

"I was just glad to do my part. And I can't thank her enough for bringing you and me together. But beyond that? I'm not so sure." Beside him, his spoon slid down the side of the bowl into a puddle of melted ice cream. Let it, he told himself while he tapped a finger against his chin. This conversation was more important.

"Well, there's Tobias Cook." Sarah polished off the last of her dessert and set her bowl aside. "He held onto her camera all those years. All the while, he hoped he'd see her again. Hanna's appearance fulfilled his lifelong dream. Then, there's Louise. Thanks to Hanna, she's a lot more trusting. Your folks learned something about their past they hadn't known before. Even the town busybody has stopped poking her nose into everyone's business."

He chuckled. "You have to admit, it's good to have people like Mrs. Jones around. She keeps everyone on their toes."

"If you say so."

Sarah's sigh told him she hadn't fully decided

where she stood on the Jones issue yet. He let it ride, taking a moment to enjoy the peace and quiet of the summer evening with the woman he loved. The first stars appeared in the night sky. Across the field, one of the dairy cows lowed.

"Did you ever figure out what happened to her? Hanna, I mean." Sarah unfolded her legs to rest her calves on the next step.

Momentarily distracted by the view, he allowed himself one good, long look before he took a breath and plunged ahead. "At first, I couldn't figure out why there wasn't a missing person report. Even after all this time, our records that far back are pretty good. But then I read something in one of Tobias's books that made me think hours and minutes measure differently in different time periods. In 2016, Hanna spent six days with us, but in 1945, she might have only been gone a day. Maybe two. Plus, there was the blizzard—it's still on record as producing one of the biggest snowfalls Central Falls has ever had in December. I imagine it took a few days for everyone to dig out, get life back to normal. By then, she was home, in her own time again."

"It's all a little, what did your dad call it—woo-woo?" Sarah rocked her hand back and forth. "But it sounds right, considering everything we know."

"Yeah, amazing, right? Who would have thought, time travel in Central Falls?" It still boggled his mind. "We know for sure that Chet made it home. He was in Malmedy—Hanna was right about that—but a handful survived. He was one of them. According to his service record, he was taken in by the French Resistance. They hid him from the Germans until the war ended in Europe."

"But he made it?" Sarah asked with a catch in her voice.

"He did, indeed." He snugged her close. "From what I've been able to piece together, he arrived back in Central Falls a day or two before Christmas." He paused for a moment, imagining Chet and Hanna's joyful reunion.

Sarah rested her head on his shoulder. "And later? What happened to them after that?"

"That had me stymied for a long time. My only clue was the postcard Hanna sent Dottie. She said she'd finally made it to the 'big city,' but I couldn't find any record of her in either New York or Boston. Today, I found out why." He reached into his shirt pocket for the newspaper article that had come across his desk that morning. After nothing turned up on Chet or Hanna in the closest cities, he'd expanded his search throughout the United States and Europe. It had taken six months, but he'd finally hit pay dirt. He held out the paper so Sarah could see it in the light that spilled through the screen door.

"An obituary?" She lifted one eyebrow. "In French?"

"Hanna's and Chet's. My high school French is a little rusty, but if I'm reading this right, they died within hours of each other during an influenza outbreak in 2009."

"Oh, that's so sad," Sarah said, her voice muted. She squeezed his hand. "Are you okay?"

He captured her fingers in his and pressed a kiss onto her knuckles. "They had more than fifty years together. That's something to be thankful for. From all accounts, they had a good life." Once he'd had the obituary, the rest had been easy to track down. "They emigrated to France, to Paris, right after the war. I suppose Chet wanted to repay the people who'd saved him from the Germans. After a few months in the city, they bought a bombed-out winery just outside of Orleans, at the north end of the Loire Valley. That area was hit hard during the war. They rebuilt, replanted, and opened a home for war orphans."

"That makes sense." Sarah gazed toward the house on the hill above them. "Hanna was so good with Gwennie." She turned toward him. "Did they have children of their own?"

"I'm not sure yet. Most of their estate passed to a foundation that uses the proceeds from the winery to fund relief efforts for children in war-torn areas across the globe, but there's a Pierre Morse on their Board of Directors. Morse is a common name, though. I'll have to do a little more digging."

"So, their legacy continues." Sarah inhaled sharply. "Just think how many lives they touched, all because you helped her get back to her own time."

The thought that he'd played some small role in making a difference for so many warmed him from the inside out. Thanks to Hanna, he'd accomplished far more than he'd set out to do.

Sarah propped her arms on the boards behind her and leaned back. "Do you think she remembered, you know, anything about being here?"

He'd given that very question a lot of thought. He'd even caught himself eyeing senior citizens, wondering if this was the day an aged Hanna would walk back into their lives. When she didn't show up, though, he'd decided that she hadn't retained any memory of the time she'd spent in the future. Now, having seen their obituary, he had to rethink that idea. Unfolding the page, he showed Sarah the photo at the bottom of the lengthy article. Just looking at it sent shivers racing down his back.

Eager to see whether she'd have the same reaction, he bent forward as she studied the photograph of an elderly couple standing before a roaring fire at Christmas. Hanna's round cheeks were lined but her blue eyes still sparkled. In the black-and-white print, it was hard to tell, but her hair looked lighter. He guessed it had whitened. It still curled softly about her shoulders, though—that hadn't changed.

But the room had drawn his attention and refused to let go. Two couches in a floral print faced each other in front of the elderly couple. A crooked chimney broom had been propped on the hearth. Checkered drapes had been pulled open to reveal wide windows that overlooked a vineyard. Garland tied with shiny ribbons adorned the window sills. Behind Hanna and

Chet, a replica of a barn sat on the mantel over the fireplace. Leafy vines and grapes had been carved into the pillars on either side.

"This could be your parents' living room," Sarah pointed out.

"I thought the same thing when I saw it," he said with a quiver in his voice. Whether Hanna could clearly recall the few days she spent in 2016 or not, the two rooms were too eerily similar to explain away as a mere coincidence.

"What's that?" Sarah pointed to a plaque that hung high on the chimney.

"The winery's crest, I think." He studied the three P's arranged in a wreath of olive branches over a banner.

"Hey, I recognize that symbol." Sarah straightened. "I'm pretty sure I've seen it on a wine bottle." She traced one finger over the banner. "La Plus Petite Pierre," she read aloud.

"'The smallest stone,'" he said. At Sarah's perplexed expression, he explained. "That's the translation. La Plus Petite Pierre, the smallest stone."

"Makes a ripple," she finished in a voice filled with wonder.

He gathered up their dishes. "Come on. I picked up a bottle on my way home today so we could try it out." But if he'd expected Sarah to jump at the chance to try the high-end burgundy, he'd misjudged her. "What?" he asked when she stayed put.

"No wine for me." She slid a hand over her midsection.

"Is your stomach still bothering you?" Here, he'd

been rambling on and on while she was under the weather. Could he be any more insensitive? He vowed to pay better attention. "Never mind the wine for now. It can wait till you're up for it."

"It could be a while," she warned.

"How long?" Something in her tone sent a ripple of unease down his back. An empty, hollow space opened up in the pit of his stomach.

Did Sarah have more than a simple stomach bug? Was she *ill*?

His thoughts scrambled. He'd promised her *in sickness and in health*, and he'd meant it. "Whatever it is, we'll get through it together," he said, swearing to move heaven and earth, do anything to help her get well. "Have you seen Dr. Lipscomb?"

"I have an appointment next week. But I have a pretty good idea that there won't be any alcohol in my immediate future." A mischievous smile stretched across Sarah's face. "At least, not for the next nine months or so."

"Nine?" He gulped. *So, this is what it feels like to go weak in the knees.* It was a good thing he was already sitting or he'd be tumbling head over teakettle down the steps. "Are you saying… ?"

"Yeah, we are." Sarah's smile danced in her eyes.

A baby. He was going to be a father. Sarah, a mother.

"Well, that's…" He struggled to find the right word. "Amazing. Wonderful. The best news I've heard all week. All month." He gave Sarah a sheepish smile. "Ever."

"So, what do you want? A boy or a girl?"

"Either. Both." He laughed. Sobering, he met Sarah's earnest gaze. "As long as you and the baby are healthy, I don't care."

She rested her head on his shoulder. "What do you think of 'Tobias' if it's a boy?"

Truth be told, he liked that just fine. He closed his eyes and pictured a future that included playing catch in the back yard with little Toby, going to high school football games on Friday nights, passing along the love for the land that had been handed down from his father. Of course, this baby might not be a boy, and he was fine with that, too. Girls meant tea parties and frilly dresses, daddy-daughter dances and walking the floor when she was old enough to date.

He tipped his head to Sarah's and smiled. "And if it's a girl, what should we name her?"

"I think we should name her Hanna," whispered Sarah. Newspaper rustled as she traced her finger in a circle around the picture of Chet and Hanna, who stood, holding hands in front of the fire. "One of these days, that's going to be us."

"Whatever the future holds for us, I can't wait." He leaned forward to kiss the woman of his dreams, the mother of his child.

The future was theirs. Now was the time to live it.

"Yes!"

Gingerbread Cupcakes with Christmas Comet Cookies

A Hallmark Original Recipe

In *Journey Back to Christmas*, the comet only comes around once every seventy-one years, but you can make this cupcake and cookie combo any time. The recipe takes the old-fashioned tradition of gingerbread and gives it a modern twist. Like a comet, this dessert is a spectacular sight, and it tastes just as good as it looks.

Yield: 18 cupcakes
Prep Time: 1 hour
Bake Time: 10 minutes
Total Time: 2 hours

INGREDIENTS

Gingerbread Cookies:

- ½ cup (1 stick) butter, softened
- ½ cup dark brown sugar, packed
- 2 teaspoons each: ground ginger and cinnamon
- ¾ teaspoon each: ground cloves and salt
- 1 egg, large
- ½ cup molasses
- 3 cups flour
- ½ teaspoon baking soda
- ¼ teaspoon baking powder

Cream Cheese Buttercream Frosting:

- 1 (8-ounce) package cream cheese, softened
- ½ cup (1 stick) unsalted butter, softened
- 4 cups powdered sugar
- 1 tablespoon vanilla extract
- 1 teaspoon grated orange zest (optional)
- As needed, white royal icing in pastry bag
- 18 gingerbread cupcakes, prepared (from scratch or baking mix)
- As needed, gold and white sparkling sugar sprinkles

DIRECTIONS

1. To prepare gingerbread cookies: cream butter and sugar in the bowl of a stand mixer until fluffy. Add spices, egg and molasses; mix to blend. Combine dry ingredients in a separate bowl; slowly add to mixing bowl on low speed until fully blended. Pat dough into 2 cookie dough disks. Cover and chill for 1 hour.

2. Preheat oven to 350 degrees F.

3. Roll 1 cookie dough disk out on a floured surface to ⅛-to ¼-inch thick, lifting and turning dough as you roll (reserve remaining cookie dough for another use). Cut out shapes with comet/shooting star-shaped cookie cutter. Transfer to baking sheets lined with parchment. Bake for 8 to 10 minutes, or until slightly light brown around outer edges. Cool.

4. To prepare frosting: combine cream cheese and butter in bowl of stand mixer and mix until fully blended. Slowly add powdered sugar until blended; add vanilla and orange zest and mix until smooth and creamy.

5. Pipe royal icing around outer edges of cookies, if desired.

6. Frost cupcakes with offset spatula or piping bag. Sprinkle sparkling sugar over frosting and top each cupcake with a gingerbread comet cookie.

Thanks so much for reading *Journey Back to Christmas*. We hope you enjoyed it!

You might also like these other books from Hallmark Publishing:

Christmas in Homestead
Love You Like Christmas
A Heavenly Christmas
A Dash of Love
Moonlight in Vermont
Love Locks

For information about our new releases and exclusive offers, sign up for our free newsletter at hallmarkchannel.com/hallmark-publishing-newsletter

You can also connect with us here:

Facebook.com/HallmarkPublishing

Twitter.com/HallmarkPublish

CHRISTMAS IN HOMESTEAD

Kara Tate

CHAPTER ONE

As Jessica McEllis rode in the back of her custom, tinted-window town car to her home in a chic, gated community of Los Angeles, she rested easy in knowing exactly how blessed she was to have the life she did.

It was what she'd been working toward for years, and now all her dreams were coming true. She was at the top of her game as an actress and about to start her new adventure and climb the next rung on her career ladder: Producer.

She'd strived to get here and, well, so what if she'd given up certain things to achieve her dreams? No one got everything they wanted.

But, a little privacy would be nice occasionally. Sometimes she felt... tired.

Like right now as she returned from a meeting with her agent.

As her driver-slash-bodyguard-slash-superhero, Gavin, pulled up to the gate of her posh home, he had to slow down to avoid hitting the gaggle of paparazzi hoping to catch a good shot of her and maybe even a word or two.

Sure, sometimes the fame could take a toll in a way Jessica had never expected. But it was that same fame and success that enabled her to pick and choose which stories she wanted to tell. And this new movie was her most exciting venture yet.

The car rolled to a stop to let the gate slip open.

"Jessica! Jessica!" The photo-shooting life-chasers were respectful enough to not get aggressive and pound on the car.

They'd always treated her well—or as well as you could treat someone whose life you used to get paid. She tried to remember they were just doing their job and to handle them fairly in return. Hollywood was a tough world. She got it. She didn't have to like it, but she got it.

After all, not many people had the opportunities and lifestyle these compromises afforded her. She traveled the world, met interesting people, and posed for some of the top photographers. Dealing with paparazzi was just the other part of the job description.

Focusing on the good in her life helped her smile through the invasion of her privacy. It was what she did. Every day. Jess placed the camera-ready, friendly grin on her face as she lowered the window.

"Hi, guys. Good to see you, as always." She did a quick scan of the group, filled with the usual suspects and a few more hoping to grab a great shot of her before the new movie.

"Jessica!" Ian Carter, who had always been ambitious but kind, shouted, waving his free hand to get her attention. "We saw Vince Hawkins arrive. What's it like doing another film with your ex-boyfriend?"

She'd known that would be a popular question when she'd cast her ex in the role of the innkeeper to her movie star. Star-crossed lovers of the modern type. She just hadn't thought she'd hear the same question quite this often.

She was also for world peace, against global warming, and pro-classic pencil skirts, but no one ever asked her about those.

"*Ex*-boyfriend, guys. Keyword here is *ex*." She gave them her best sassy grin to let them know it was all in fun—no hard feelings—then sent the focus back to where she wanted it: the movie. "It's going to be a great film."

And that was all that mattered. She'd agreed to bring Vince on because they worked well together and had amazing on-screen chemistry. She needed the best chance at success she could get with her first film as a producer and was willing to take whatever measures she had to. Even if that meant dealing with the celebrity gossip hounds creating un-stories about her and her co-star.

She flashed the photographers another warm smile and started to roll up her window before giving them all a little wave. The continued shouts of her name echoed in the car as she collapsed back against the rich leather seats. It was time to put her producer hat on now that she'd gotten her actress duties out of the way.

"Gavin." She leaned forward to talk to her bodyguard as he pulled up to her front door. "We're definitely heading into new territory with this one."

He flashed her a wide smile in the rearview mirror and nodded his agreement.

Oh, Gavin. You chatty fellow, you.

Before getting out of the car, she straightened her skirt and pulled it as low as she could. She had no interest in being the next accidental flasher and going viral with her panties showing. Those super-powered lenses meant always being hyper-cognizant. That awareness had become second nature. One slip-up early in her career, when she'd accidentally tucked her skirt into her panties and had ended up on a celebrity gossip site, had trained her well.

Gavin came around and opened the door, doing his best to screen her from view as she slid out. As shields went, Gavin was more like a wall, actually. Standing over six feet two inches, his bulk was intimidating enough. But his drown-in-them dark brown eyes and gorgeous smile made him look like the action star version of a bodyguard as much as the real deal.

All this had made him the obvious choice to play her bodyguard in the new movie.

The look Gavin had given her had said it all. His gift with looks was particularly helpful since Gavin was a man of few words. Actually, most of the time, he was a man of *no* words.

Jessica gave another wave down the drive and headed toward the house, pulling off her hat as she went. It was good to be home. Her house was a sanctuary. The true center of her world away from prying eyes and being Public Jessica. Everything how she liked it, clean lines, organized. A place where she had complete control.

A place where there was suddenly a huge, beautifully decorated Christmas tree.

Behind her, Gavin stopped, obviously taking in the new addition as well. At least, she'd like to think he was wondering what in the world it was doing in her living room, since that was exactly what she was thinking.

"Jess!" Rosalie, her publicist, stood, Christmas ball in hand, in front of the room's new addition. "What do you think?"

"Rosalie, what is that?" Jessica motioned to the tree, even though she was pretty sure Rosalie must know the huge pine-scented thing in her living room was the obvious issue.

"It's a Christmas tree." Rosalie flashed her a stunning smile and waved the ornament in her hand a bit before finding a home for it on the tree.

"Yes." Well, ask a silly question… "It's beautiful. Why is it in my house?"

Rosalie set the next decoration down and turned to Jessica. She continued to smile, but it looked a bit forced. "Because it's almost Christmas." She waved a hand toward the tree, beautiful and perfect, just like all of Rosalie's handiwork. "Everyone needs a tree."

Jessica glanced around and couldn't help feeling like she was killing the joy as she wondered why in the world she needed a tree. In *her* house. Rosalie had obviously taken great care with it, creating a masterpiece any celebrity magazine would be more than thrilled to add to their holiday spreads.

But still.

Jess stepped into the room, joining Rosalie, and placed a hand on her shoulder, trying to lessen the sting of her response.

"We're spending the next ten days in Iowa shooting a Christmas movie. I'll see plenty of trees there."

"Yeah, but…" Rosalie glanced over her shoulder and lowered her voice. "You're producing and starring in the movie. How much tree-enjoyment, holiday-spirit time will you get?"

"Probably a lot, since it's a Christmas movie." And again, Iowa. Lots of trees.

"Okay." Rosalie shook her head, obviously not letting go of her hope of a Holiday Spirit taking over the event. "Your co-star awaits you for the meeting. Barbara just texted. She's two minutes away."

Not exactly what Jessica wanted to hear. Things went smoothly when people were on time. Plans mattered. Plans got things done, and being a strong planner had gotten her this far—producing at thirty wasn't something to sneeze at.

"Thanks. But a director who runs late…" She shook it off. No reason to get off on the wrong foot. Barbara was a pro, and she'd make it work. "Okay, let's do this so I can pack and get on the road."

Rosalie gave a little shake of her head, probably laughing at Jessica's need for order. "I'll wait for Barbara."

Which was exactly what Jessica needed. She had other issues to deal with, and it was probably best to handle them without an audience—especially an audience completely made up of the movie's future director.

She took a deep breath and went to handle Vince Hawkins, Mr. Hollywood's Most Eligible Bachelor—at least, he was since their breakup. Hopefully, they'd work together with the same magic they'd had before.

And if not, she'd figure that out, too.

In the game room at the back of the house, she found him playing billiards by himself—and, of course, dressed like a *GQ* fashion shoot was happening around him.

He glanced up, giving her a once-over.

"That's a nice tree upstairs." He flashed her his signature smile. "Whose is it?"

"What do you mean, whose is it?" She tried not to get defensive, but leave it to Vince to rock the boat as soon as she walked in the room. "It's mine."

"Yeah, right." Vince gave her a look that clearly stated he didn't even believe her a little bit before sending yet another one of his grins her way. "Since when do you get a tree?"

The need to justify her unwanted tree had her digging in her heels. It was in her house, it was Christmas, and she was not going to let Vince come in here and make her feel defensive.

"Since— Well, I felt like it."

"Ah." Vince leaned against the billiards table, going into full flirt mode. "But who needs a tree when they'll be in Fiji again for Christmas with… ?"

He drew the word out, and Jessica knew exactly what he was getting at. Vince seemed to be having a rough time letting go of this dating relationship. He was treating the pre-production meetings like business as usual for them.

But it wasn't. Not even a little. They were friends now—*just* friends—and she needed him to get that. She had wanted more than what their relationship had offered. They both deserved more, even as she still valued the friendship they'd developed before they'd changed it to a romantic one.

"Her best girlfriend?" Jessica tried not to roll her eyes and placed a hand on Vince's arm. "Vince, you and I broke up. Jill is going to Fiji in your place this year."

She kept having to have these conversations with him.

He'd even told one media outlet two months ago they were just on a break.

"Ouch." He winced. "Good for Jill, though."

He took a step closer, forcing Jess to stand her ground as he shifted right back into handsome-leading-man persona.

Before she could swing them into work mode, he went on. "So, does that mean we should keep things strictly professional on location?"

That was a bud to nip immediately, and not just because of the no-longer-dating part of the conversation.

"This is my first time producing a movie." She tried to keep the nerves out of her voice. Vince would do an amazing job and have her back, but she wanted to be confident, professional—and taken seriously. "My first big thing after the *Asterlight* series, and I can't let anything mess that up."

"Classic Jessica." Vince added a smirk to his nod.

"What does that mean?" Coming from Vince, that definitely didn't sound like a compliment.

"You always have a detailed plan for everything."

Again, not a compliment.

"No, I don't." Okay, maybe she did. But that wasn't a bad thing.

Vince had accused her more than once of being a control freak who made him live by her detailed plans.

"Do so!"

She took a step back. Five-year-olds had more mature arguments than this.

"Well, excuse me, Mr. Play-everything-by-ear." She squared her shoulders, trying to make herself bigger to match his size and ability to loom over her. Not that he'd ever use that advantage on her. Vince was secretly a teddy bear.

They'd always bickered. It was often how they communicated. But, while Cary Grant and Katharine Hepburn were adorable when they did it on-screen, it wasn't always as much fun off-screen.

He paused, leaning into her space.

"You know,"—Vince grinned, waggling his eyebrows a bit—"if this were a movie, this would be the part where we kiss."

"Do you see a camera?" She was *so* done with this conversation.

He flipped his phone out of his pocket with a not-so-subtle, "Bam!" and another waggle of the brows. Jessica shook her head, smiling. Vince wasn't just a charmer, he was truly charming. He'd always known how to lighten her moods. It was one of the balances that made them a good team.

"Come on. Truce?" He tapped a finger on his cheek. "It will be good PR for the movie."

Jess rolled her eyes. There he went pushing exactly the right buttons again to get her to do what he wanted. The movie's success was vital to her. She loved the story and was proud to make this her first producer gig.

"Fine." She leaned into to kiss his cheek, surprised—and yet on some level, not—when he turned his head at the last second and snapped the pic. "Vince!"

Vince flashed her a grin, that smile that let him get

away with too much for too long from way too many people. "This will look great on Instagram."

"That is not funny." This was the last thing she needed while trying to juggle all the other pre-production tasks and meetings. A personal PR nightmare. "I'm not kidding. Delete that."

"Oh, come on."

"No." Jess knew when to put her foot down. With Vince, that was pretty much always.

He gave her a long look then shook his head as if he were thinking about it before flashing that get-away-with-anything grin again.

"Fine." Vince flipped to the pic, holding it up for her to see with his other hand.

She should have known better than to just walk away.

Read the rest! *Christmas in Homestead* is available now.